B O O

BREAK OF THE SIX

MATT RYAN

THE PRESTON SIX SERIES

For information on new releases
or if you want to chat with me, you can find me at:
www.facebook.com/authormattryan
or www.authormattryan.com

Cover: Regina Wamba
www.maeidesign.com
Editor: Victoria Schmitz | Crimson Tide Editorial
Formatting: Inkstain Interior Book Designing
www.inkstainformatting.com

BOOKS BY MATT RYAN

Rise of the Six
Call of the Six
Fall of the Six
Break of the Six

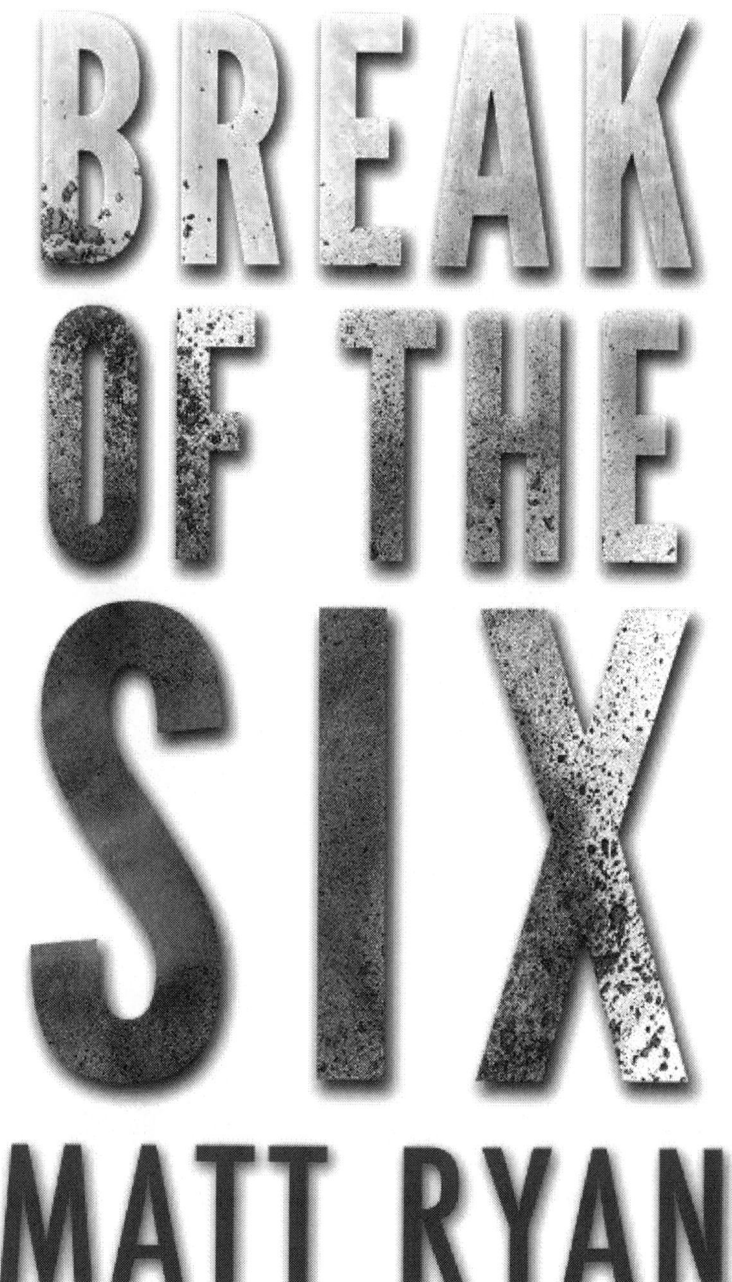

THE PRESTON SIX SERIES

CHAPTER 1

SAMANTHA BRUSHED HER HAIR OVER her shoulder as she walked past the metal detector. The guard eyed her up and down and she rolled her eyes. If he tried to give her another pat down, she'd be telling Zach. Her scowl must have worked because he waved her on. She couldn't understand why so much security would be needed for a company based on medical research. Guess there were a lot of wackos in San Francisco.

The elevator took her to the sixteenth floor. Veronica, the receptionist, eyed her as she exited the elevator. The girl didn't like her. Many of the people on the sixteenth floor didn't like her, but who cared. She earned her way to the top, whether they believed it or not. They could be jealous if they wanted.

She strutted past Veronica and toward her corner office, pausing to admire her name etched in glass over the door. It seemed as far away from Preston as she could get and that's exactly what she needed. It was her nineteenth birthday today and she couldn't help but wonder if the group was meeting at Joey's as they always had.

She flung the door open and was already mad for letting herself think about her past. She wouldn't allow herself to think of them and the perfect couple again. Taking a deep breath, Samantha straightened her posture and marched by her desk. She ran a finger over the smooth wood top on her way to the windows. She loved the view. Not a tree in sight, only a parking lot and a grass field beyond. At night, the city lit up the horizon so it always felt like the sun might be coming over the hill at any moment.

Someone tapped on her door. She looked back at the noise and saw Zach Baker standing just outside the doorway. The man owned the entire building, yet still knocked and waited to be invited in. She motioned and he entered. She took a moment to take in his fantastic suit. The blue tie had a large tie clip with an elegant black stone in the middle.

The man was gorgeous. A lean, muscular guy, not much older than her. Well, she thought he wasn't, she actually hadn't asked him his age yet. She cleared her throat and kept her eyes on his. It took her months to build up to maintaining eye contact with the man.

"Doing okay? You seemed a bit upset coming in today."

Did he miss nothing? She'd never told him anything about her past, or the Preston Six, and certainly nothing about other worlds. Talk about stuff like that and he'd surely think she was crazy and put her back on floor one. "Nothing, just thinking about my past."

"Your past brought you here. I thank your past for that gift."

Samantha sighed and got lost in his smile. He had such a youthful look, but his eyes held wisdom. "Well, sometimes the past sucks."

Zach laughed. "Yes, it does." He paused. "I came to see you because I want to show you something."

Samantha's curiosity piqued. He left the room and she eagerly followed him toward the elevator, making sure to share a joke as they passed by Veronica. She'd show that bitch who had his attention.

They entered the elevator and Zach put a card in a slot on the wall. "This will get us to floor seventeen."

"So it's real."

"Very much so."

Rumors swirled of a research floor, but Samantha hated rumors and wanted to deal in facts; she needed to see it before believing it. Believing in false realities is what ultimately led her to leave Preston.

The elevator doors closed and Zach turned to her. "Have you heard of the cough that's going around?"

"Yeah, I've heard a few things on the news about it. Is it something we're working on?"

"I don't think anyone knows how dangerous it is yet." He took on a serious tone with fire in his eyes.

She had to stop looking at him, he was the boss. *He is asking about the cough*, she reminded herself. "They say it isn't fatal, just a new strain of bronchitis or something." Samantha didn't want to admit she barely knew anything about it.

The elevator doors slid open and Zach motioned for her to exit first. Attached to the elevator was a small glass room. "Decontamination chamber, just be a minute while it gets rid of any germs." He winked. Normally such behavior would be a red flag, but he had such an easy way to him, as stupid as it sounds, she found it charming.

Samantha turned in a circle and felt the puffs of air pelting her body. Many people in white jumpsuits moved around in the room beyond. Spinning vials, bubbling bottles, and many white, boxy electronics scattered around the sterile looking environment.

"Have I told you what a pleasure it is to have you working for me?" Zach asked. His playful tone was back.

She almost missed the intensity he briefly showed her in the elevator. How many layers did he have behind those eyes? "Thank you, but to be honest, I'm not sure how much I've contributed."

"Someone as special as you, is deserving of a special task."

"You keep flattering me this way, Mr. Baker, and I'll think I'm too good for this job." He laughed. It was infectious and she laughed with him. She resisted the urge to touch his arm and held her hand tight to her side. A bell dinged and a green light lit above the glass door.

"We're all clear." Zach opened the door, dipping his head close to her ear. "And, when we're alone, Samantha . . . it's Zach."

A shiver ran down her spine as his breath ran over her cheek. *He's your boss.*

Making a quick tour of the floor, he took his time to explain the various things they were working on. She didn't have a clue about most of what he was talking about, until he brought her to a computer displaying a twisted helix.

"As I said, I don't think the world knows what it really is, but I can assure you, the CDC is taking this very serious. Luckily, we've found what the medical world is fervently searching for." He pointed at the screen.

Samantha leaned in closer to the 3D model. "What is it?"

He brushed her arm as he typed into the keyboard. The contact sent another chill down her arm. A man hadn't made her feel anything like that since . . . *No*. She wouldn't allow herself to think about it. Never again, she was a new woman now—a businesswoman.

"The cause of the Cough."

The news started calling it that because all the people who had it coughed, a lot. It was some kind of new virus that irritated your lungs, but most were saying it wasn't dangerous. Just a new strain of the common cold.

Samantha raised an eyebrow. "I didn't know we were even looking into it."

"I've been doing this in my spare time, but I found something—something terrible." The fire crept back in his eyes and she froze under their glare. "I don't want to scare you but, Samantha, this is going to be an epidemic. These people are going to die."

She stood straight up. "What?" She must've heard him wrong and kept shaking her head, waiting for his correction.

"The first death happened today. They're running the story tonight."

"How can you know this?"

He grinned, and then a dangerous look spread across his face. A look she felt could consume her whole. "I have a few contacts."

She swallowed and wondered if she was getting in over her head with Zach. "What can we do?"

"You've enjoyed working here, correct?"

"Yes, very much so." Almost as much as she enjoyed not being in Preston.

"I'm very happy to hear that because I've watched you over the last year. I think you're ready to take on a big task. What do you think?"

"I..." She held her hand over her mouth. She wanted a task, an important one. Something she could shove down all the throats of floor sixteen. Maybe she could even show the remnants of Preston how far she'd come. "I'm ready."

"Good, because I started this company to change the world and I think this is our opportunity to do exactly that. What if I told you that soon we'll have a cure—a vaccine—for the Cough?" She began to ask a question, but he pushed forward. "And what if I wanted you to be the one to announce it to the world and see that it gets delivered?"

Samantha's mouth hung open, fear crashing over her. She strained to get the words out, but her throat constricted. She could barely breathe.

Zach placed his soft hand on her shoulder, tracing circles along her bare skin. "Samantha, this is the special mission I have for you. You're going to be the face of the cure. And I won't let you fail, I'll be right behind you the whole time."

She closed her mouth and placed her hand on top of his. She felt strength in those hands. A new wave of fear crashed against her as the realization of what he was saying hit her full force. The world had a deadly virus attacking it and didn't even know it yet. Preston, what would happen there? She felt her free hand touching her phone in her black slacks.

"Not yet." He gazed at her phone. "No one can know about what we are doing until we have it ready. I'll make sure your hometown, Preston, right?" She nodded. "We'll make sure they are on the first delivery list."

She tapped her phone and wanted to warn them. She hadn't spoken to any of them in a year and she wasn't even sure if they were even still in Preston. They could be anywhere in the worlds.

CHAPTER 2

THE CROWD CHANTED POLY'S NAME. That in and of itself wasn't the weird thing though . . . it was that she had gotten used to it. She had a few goosebumps on her arm as she stood next to Jonathan and Julie, but she didn't feel like throwing up anymore. After two weeks of traveling around Vanar, opening orange centers and having new net centers named after them, she felt like she was becoming a pro at awkwardly accepting praise and admiration. Though, she was starting to miss Earth, and more specifically, Preston.

Walking toward the front of the stage, they cheered her name louder. Poly glanced at Travis, standing near his building with Gladius at his side. They hadn't had a chance to discuss what Julie had found, but she knew the ceremony would be short, followed with a party. They'd talk then.

"Yes, Poly, Poly, Poly!" Jonathan chanted with the masses through his microphone. As she came up to his side, he raised his hands and settled the crowd down to silence. "I'm not going to sugar coat things, people of Sanct, we've been through hell over the last year. Many of us have lost loved ones, and even worse, we've developed wrinkles." Jonathan pointed to the crow's feet at the corner of his eyes.

Poly looked out as laughter spread through the crowd. Sanct had once been a playland for the rich and beautiful. Now, the shine had left the faces of its people, and the buildings wrapping around the circular city looked dull and lackluster. Only a few scattered windows had lights on and the traffic, once bustling, now halted to almost nothing but a few airships.

She and her friends stood on a stage right in front of Travis's newly erected building. What made it stand out was the fact it didn't. The plain beige walls with functional windows looked like an ordinary building and only reached half the height of his old one.

Jonathan grabbed Poly around the shoulders and flashed his charming smile. His teeth weren't as shiny as before, but she preferred the natural look versus the freakishly bright white.

"It has been over a year since MM seized this city, stopped the production of orange, and took away our networks." The crowd booed.

He let go of Poly and looked at the wooden stage below his feet. "These things seem so insignificant now," he said. "Remember when our biggest problem was a lag on our network, or whether or not the food printer was going to give you diarrhea?" The crowd laughed again, but Jonathan didn't perk up to the reception. He continued looking at the stage and shook his head. After a short silence, charm spread over his face as he regarded the crowd.

"In this rare day of celebration, our president opens his new building, marking a new age of ugly architecture." He pointed at Travis and laughed. "I'm sorry, Travis, uh . . . Mr. President, but did you get a discount on beige?"

Travis laughed and rubbed a beige wall with his hand. "Its beauty will be in its function, not in its appearance." The crowd cheered for Travis as he stepped away from the wall, waving to the crowd. "This building is but a step in getting us back to where we once were." He shook his head. "No. Not where we were, but to even a better place, because we won't have the noose around our neck. Marcus Malliden will play God with our lives no longer."

Poly knew this would draw a huge reaction from the crowd and it did. She couldn't help but smile at Travis. He seemed to have such a way with politics and crowds, it was no wonder he beat out Harris in the elections.

He walked toward Poly and she felt Joey nudging closer, even clasping her hand with his. She wanted to laugh, but knew he didn't like Travis getting too close. Joey smiled at the crowd and she knew how he loved the reactions she got from the world of Vanar. He said they loved her and he could relate to that. She squeezed his hand and never felt happier to have him by her side, to experience life together.

"This little lady," Travis said, squeezing her shoulder, "not to mention Joey, Lucas, Julie, and Hank, all sacrificed so much to rid us of Marcus."

Lucas pulled the microphone. "Don't forget about Harris." He waved to the crowd, amused by his own comment and the crowd's thunderous applause.

Travis pursed his lips, then smoothed out his face. "I suppose . . . Harris did his part too." He struggled to get the words out. "Poly, would you do the honor of cutting the ceremonial ribbon?"

Gladius rushed across the stage with Gem following close behind, both wearing tiny white dresses with a thin red line right below the bust. She carried an oversized pair of scissors and smiled as she approached. "I had Douglas sharpen them up this time, should cut like razor blades."

Poly took the scissors and walked to the large ribbon stretching past the front door. The crowd went silent with anticipation. This was her fourth ribbon cutting and she felt silly each time. Who was she to be cutting anything? But the crowd seemed to be leaning forward, waiting for the cut. It was considered bad luck if she didn't get a clean slice on the first try. She learned this after the fiasco ribbon cutting at the last orange center opening.

With Joey and her friends at her side, she slid the ribbon between the blades and squeezed the handles in as she pushed them together. The ribbon sliced in two and floated to the ground. She giggled at the crowd's applause. A pulse of music sounded above and the crowd continued to roar to its beat.

"Nicely done, Poly," Jonathan yelled over the noise and then pointed to the sky. "Now, for your entertainment pleasure, we have DJ Black Hole."

The DJ arrived from above, floating on a disc that pulsated with a deep bass beat. She knew the song from the club she and

Julie had gone to with Travis. The crowd began to dance and rock out to the electric drive.

Travis drew them in closer. "How about I give you a tour of the new building?"

"Yes, please do," Poly said and they all made their way toward the front doors and away from the music.

Gladius walked next to her and leaned in. "I see you still have the cute one snatched up." She eyed Joey, lingering on his butt. "If I don't make a pick soon, all these boys will be gobbled up by your lot." Once she'd learned about Earth and the stones, she changed from surly to friendly. Fascinated by the knowledge of other worlds, she would grill Julie and Poly about what Earth was like. And with increasing certainty, Poly thought she even wanted an Earth boy for herself.

Laughing, Poly said, "This one's mine." She pulled Joey closer to her.

"Hey, Gladius." Joey nodded his head in greeting. "I like your dress."

"Thanks." She winked at Poly and laughed. "If you ever get tired of this one, you let me know." They followed Travis into the building and the sounds of DJ Black Hole were muted, falling to a continuous thud of electric music.

"I swear I am going to go crazy if I can't figure out the compression you guys use on your digital files. There is no music that awesome on Earth," Julie said, scanning her Panavice.

Travis showed them the bland lobby and must have seen their lack of amazement at a receptionist's desk. Getting on the elevator, he pressed the floor thirty-two button. "Thanks for coming," he said, looking at Poly. "All of you. I don't think you know how much it means for the people to see your faces.

Gladius even wrote up a well-written article about your importance to Vanar. It has spread over much of the world."

Poly glanced at Gladius, who for once in her life shrunk away from the attention.

Travis laughed. "If I could, I'd have you all living here with me."

"We're pretty happy on Earth," Joey said and put his arm around Poly. She loved when he pulled her close.

"What's the status on getting your net back up?" Julie asked.

The elevator stopped and the doors slid open. "Not good, Alice destroyed much of the systems around the world. My net people said this year for Sanct, but I fear the rest of the world will be far behind. Harris is building net drones to provide the net to further reaches of the world as well."

Hank coughed as he left the elevator. "You okay, big guy?" Gladius patted him on the back as he kept coughing. She hit him so hard, Poly thought about saying something, but Hank just smiled.

"I'm fine, just a bit of a dry throat."

Gem ran past Poly to what she thought was Gladius's new desk, but Douglas sat behind it now. He shrieked and pushed away from Gem as it got behind the desk with him. The doll waddled out from behind the desk, holding a bottle of water. It looked huge in its tiny hands as it staggered over to Gladius.

"Gem, you are such a sweetheart." Gladius plucked the water bottle from its arms and handed it to Hank.

"Thanks," Hank said.

"Travis, we wanted to talk to you about something we found on Earth," Poly said, looking to Julie.

"Yes," Julie took over, "I believe I found him."

"Come, let's get back to my office and discuss this. Douglas, can you hold my calls and meetings for the time being?"

Douglas took a deep breath, then released it over what felt like a full minute before answering. "Fine."

Travis opened the plain white doors to his office. There were no weapons on the walls, or fancy furniture. The only thing Poly recognized was the picture of Maya sitting on the wall behind his desk.

Travis sat down in the new lounge area with a couch and many chairs surrounding it. Poly sat on one of the chairs and Joey stood behind her.

Lucas jumped on the couch and laid out next to Travis. "This is one nice couch."

"Thanks," Travis said. "So, what did you find, Julie?"

"I can get into any system on Earth with ease, until I found something that looked very familiar to MM's old security protocols on a server. I danced at the edges of it, but I knew it was him. There isn't another person on the planet who would have a system like that."

"Tell him the worst part," Hank said.

"The company that has this system is ZRB, which is also the same company were our friend, Samantha, is currently employed."

"Samantha . . . I'm sorry I never got to meet her. Are you sure of this?"

"Without a doubt."

Travis leaned back in his chair and rubbed his chin. "What are you planning to do?"

Poly's mouth hung open. She thought maybe he might be the one suggesting a plan. Maybe an offer of some assistance to help stop the man who ruined Vanar and Ryjack.

"We don't really have a plan yet."

Hank started coughing again and took another drink from the water bottle. Gladius raised her hand to start hitting his back, but he waved her off.

"You alright there, big guy?" Travis asked.

"Yeah, just a cough."

"You know, I could have my medical staff take a look..."

"No, I'm fine," Hank said and took another swig of water.

"If I could, I would help, but we don't have the resources. If you can expose him, I will personally come to your aid."

"Dad, we can't just leave them to the whims of Marcus, the dude's a complete psycho. You know he is up to some evil shit." Gladius put her hands on her hips.

Travis regarded Julie and stood from his chair. "I'll travel to Earth when you can show me this is indeed Marcus. It is possible the company developed this technology on their own. After all, we share a similar history, it would make sense if your planet ended up developing the same technology."

"By the time Marcus shows himself, I fear it will be too late," Julie said.

"I have the same fear, but I can't leave my world on a suspicion. Get something solid, and I'll be there for you guys."

"And if he kills us before then?" Lucas asked.

Travis shook his head. "If he wanted you dead, you wouldn't be here right now. The man always has a plan."

CHAPTER 3

POLY TURNED UP THE CAR RADIO.

"The crap hit the fan and if I wasn't on the radio, I'd say a lot worse." The radio stopped playing music and had switched to a constant news feed. The DJs seemed uncomfortable discussing such a heavy subject, but what else could they do in the circumstances?

"I bet this came from terrorists, some biomedical people," the other DJ said. "You just mix influenza and small pox and bingo, pandemic."

"This is a cough..."

"But it's killing people, Jerry, this is going to kill us all if we don't get a handle on it."

Poly turned off the car radio. She hated being right, but her gut was rarely wrong. Something terrible had happened while they were gone and it covered the entire planet with panic. She gripped the steering wheel and glanced at Julie working on her Panavice. They were sick with worry, waiting for any news about Samantha. She needed to know she was okay and really wanted to grab all the family and friends she had and gather them around her.

It'd been two days since they left Travis's office and at first, the goal had been to find proof of Marcus. Then their priorities shifted when they realized all they wanted to do was get the Six back together.

When they left for Vanar, a new strain of the common cold had been on the news here and there, but now the Cough *was* the news. Every major TV channel had turned off all regular programming to concentrate on twenty-four hour coverage. A telethon had started, with a rolling list of celebrities making appearances in support of the cure. Schools were closed, along with some businesses. Preston had daily meetings on the Cough, designating groups to check in on the elderly and such. All people with symptoms were asked to head to the medical treatment center, previously known as the high school gym.

"Have you heard back from Travis?" Poly asked.

"No, he's in some area without net and Harris is MIA as well."

Poly didn't like the timing of Julie finding who they believed to be Marcus and the emergence of the Cough.

"I can't find her," Julie said.

"What do you mean, you can't find her? I thought you could find anything?" Poly said.

"I don't know, she's not leaving a digital trace anywhere."

Poly squeezed the steering wheel and glanced at Julie running her fingers over her Panavice. "We need to get the others."

"Look out!"

Poly turned to look out the windshield and slammed her foot on the brake. Hank stood in the middle of the dirt road. He jumped to the side and the car missed him by inches. As the vehicle stopped, they got out to find Hank hunched over, coughing into his fists.

"Hank, you okay?" Poly called out. Hank didn't answer but continued to cough.

"He's got it, I knew it," Julie said in a panicked fit. "The Cough."

Poly didn't want to hear it. She grabbed Hank's shoulder and shook him. "Hank!"

He knelt on the dirt, then looked up at Poly. He blinked, as if only now registering her face. "I'm okay, the walking wiped me out I guess." He put on a weak smile.

Poly put her hands over her eyes. Her mother coughed this morning but dismissed it as nothing. Poly herself felt a tickle in her throat and hoped it was just the dust swirling in the air. Hank was the first of the six to get the cough. The first she knew of at least. They'd been unable to contact Samantha.

"Come on, Hank, we can give you a lift to the town treatment center. We were on our way to get you anyway," Poly said. Hospitals were filling up so the government had stepped in to many of the worst cities and even a small town like Preston got some help with treatment centers.

"No, I don't want to infect you. I was just going to town to the," he coughed, "treatment center."

"Like we're going to leave you on the road like this." Poly and Julie helped Hank get to his feet and then into the car.

With Hank tucked away in the back seat, Poly rushed into town, only slowing down when she neared the treatment center. Cars filled the spaces and many people walked around the cars and stood in clusters outside the gym. Poly hopped over the curb and found an unused spot on the grass.

Julie raised an eyebrow.

"Let them give me a ticket," Poly said and opened the door.

Hank climbed out of the car on his own and stood at the door. "Whoa, that's a lot of people," he said before going into another coughing fit.

Poly took a deep breath and looked at the line wrapping around the outside of the gym. Many more people took to sitting on the lawn, lounging around the bike racks and loitering near the stairs to the school. She recognized some faces but many more she didn't know. It broke her heart to see so many in her home town suffering. Just yesterday, there had only been a few people near the front door. If this much changed in one day, what was going to happen over the next week?

A woman in all white stood at the front of the line. She had an American flag pin with her name under it. The government had sent these nurses here a few days ago to help set up the treatment center.

"Excuse me, I have a sick friend here," Julie called out.

"We've all got sick ones here," a man in line replied and the rest of the line grumbled in agreement.

"I'm so sorry, Frank," Poly said. "It's Hank, he's doing awful."

Frank nodded and gazed at Hank. "We're all waiting to get in, but you can go the nurse up there and have him checked in."

"Thanks."

Frank wrapped his arms around his coughing wife and nodded his head. They walked up to the nurse sitting behind a folding table. She looked up and saw Hank leaning on Julie.

"Do you know what stage he is?" the nurse asked.

Poly shook her head in confusion.

Julie stepped forward to answer. "I think he's in stage two."

"Is he coughing blood yet?"

"Hank?"

Hank shook his head, which turned into a coughing fit. When he could breathe, he took his hand away from his mouth and a spatter of blood covered his palm.

The nurse got up from behind the desk and walked to Hank. "He's entering stage three, we need to take him in."

The line protested Hank's acceptance as they entered the gym. Poly stopped at the doorway, taking in the chaotic looking gym where she had once played basketball. Cots covered the gym floor while many people curled up on their beds, coughing. She put her hand over her mouth and stumbled after Hank and the nurse.

The summer heat permeated the gym and the smell of rubbing alcohol and sweat flooded her nostrils. Another nurse ran up to them with masks. They put the masks on while Hank was placed on a cot.

"I'm sorry, what's your name?" Poly asked one of the nurses.

"Sherri."

"Hello, Sherri, I'm Poly. Could you tell me what happens after stage three?"

"Honey, the only thing after stage three is the end."

Poly grabbed at her chest and stared at Hank lying on the cot. She got closer to Sherri and whispered, "How much longer does he have?"

Sherri shuffled Poly away from Hank's hearing distance and whispered, "I won't sugarcoat it for you, sweetie, your friend probably has a day or two left."

Poly wanted to fall to the floor and scream, but she just looked at Hank, tears building in her eyes. Julie saw her face and shook her head. Poly wiped her nose and opened her eyes wide, trying to dry them out. She needed to pull it together because they couldn't tell Hank. What good would it do to tell someone they'd be dead in a day?

"What can we do for him?" Poly asked.

The nurse shook her head. "There's nothing to do but make them as comfortable as possible. He is still the man you love, so make sure you treat him as such. The last thing you want to do to a person dying is stop treating them like a human." She looked around the room and her face sagged in fatigue. "It might not matter much at this point though, this whole place is going to Hell in a hand basket if we can't get more help. And this stuff is spreading like a prairie fire in October."

Poly grabbed her phone and called Joey. The conversation was quick, but she got him to promise not to come down and to tell everyone else about it. Hank had coughed the whole ride over and she didn't think the mask was going to help her or Julie anymore. If they were going to get it, they would have it already. "What can I do to help?" She tapped the nurse on the shoulder.

"Sweetie, if you can stomach it, we need blankets changed, bed pans..." The nurse looked doubtful. "If we don't get this place clean, we'll have a whole different pandemic on our hands."

Poly nodded and looked to Julie. Julie looked terrified and pulled out her Panavice—she wasn't going to be any help. Over the last year, Poly had been to Vanar several times to make appearances and hand out food and supplies to people. She'd begun to get used to seeing people suffering, but this was her home town, she knew the people on those cots.

"Can I get some gloves?" she asked.

"Sally, can you get this angel some gloves? She's gonna help out."

Poly spent the next few hours cleaning the bedpans and sheets of the patients, but in between each moment, she rushed to check on Hank. Julie never left his side. He wasn't the only person they knew on the cots. Many of the faces were familiar, some from school and others from town events.

She felt torn; she wanted to help her town, but she wanted to be at Hank's side. She needed to hold his hand and tell him everything was going to be fine. She started to regret telling Joey not to come. She'd gotten used to him being her leaning post. Just his presence would make her feel better. But if he got sick, she didn't know if she could handle it.

A woman moaned near her and reached out her hand. She coughed as Poly approached. Poly didn't recognize her pale face at first. As she got closer, she was stunned. "Mrs. Nires?" she asked.

"Poly," she sounded weak and coughed at the end.

"Mrs. Nires, I'm so sorry, what can I do for you?"

"Water," she rasped.

Poly rushed to grab a water bottle from the pallet and brought it back to her. Mrs. Nires took a drink and coughed much of it back up. Water and cough sprayed over Poly's face and body. She wanted to jump out of her skin, to run away screaming and gargle with antibacterial liquid, but she kept still. She knew if she was going to get the cough, she already had it.

"Thank you," Mrs. Nires said and the bottle in her hand tipped, spilling out.

Poly took the bottle and twisted the cap back on. She placed it at her side and looked to Hank across the room. Julie stood next to him, splitting her attention between him and her Panavice.

"Child, I put you down for ten, maybe fifteen minutes of this, and look at you still at it. Bless your heart," Sherri said, coming up behind her. Poly's phone rang. "You better answer that."

She glanced at the screen. Joey. "Hello."

"You need to leave there now. You're exposed. It's a freaking zoo here."

"Listen, Joey, I am not leaving Hank and Julie alone in this place."

A long pause. "Fine, but then I'm coming in."

"No." It was too late. He'd hung up.

In a few minutes Joey managed to get past the door nurse guards with Lucas in tow. He searched until he spotted her. He took a mask the nurse offered and rushed past the cots and people to get to her. "Where's Hank?" Joey asked as Lucas pushed up against him.

"Over there, with Julie. He's sleeping at the moment."

Lucas squinted at Hank. "Jesus, he looks terrible." He darted over to Julie.

Joey looked past Poly to Hank and ran his hand through his hair. He paced for a second before stretching his hands out and looked at the floor. "My mom's been coughing," Joey said. "She said she's not coming here though."

Poly gasped. She hated the selfish thought, but she couldn't help thinking if Karen was sick, it meant Joey would have been exposed, same as her. "Yeah, I can't blame her. All they're doing is giving some cough medicine and IV's. I don't think this thing is going to stop. We need help." Poly gave him a look of *you-know-who.*

"Harris?" he whispered.

"Yes. They might have something for this." She wanted to guarantee it, but she didn't feel as confident as she sounded.

"They aren't what they used to be."

"You know they'll help us."

"Fine, but I'm taking you with me," Joey said, and they glanced back at Hank. "I think it's the best chance he's got."

Poly agreed and they checked in with Hank before leaving. Their friend woke up and smiled in between coughs and told them good luck. Lucas said they would stay with Hank, and Julie said she would try and find out more about her leads to Marcus. She thought Marcus could be behind it all—too much of a coincidence.

They stopped by Poly's house and Joey waited in the car while she changed and took a quick shower to get the treatment center filth off her. They parked and ran through the forest to the Alius stone. The forest around the stone was still charred, but the smoke smell was gone and the undergrowth had sprouted green ferns and plants.

"You ready?" Joey asked kneeling next to the stone.

Poly took in a deep breath and placed her hand on a knife. Joey held a gun in his hand. They'd had so many terrible trips with the stone, even going to Harris's house seemed dangerous. She nodded her head and he typed in the code.

The forest changed to the old residence of Marcus Malliden. Harris had originally taken it over as his interim headquarters but as time passed, it became the base of operations for the fractured MM.

A few guards greeted them with raised guns. Once they saw who the visitors were, they lowered their weapons. Jack ran from behind the staircase. His face brightened with a smile as he greeted them. "I thought I heard the stone. Poly, Joey, what a great surprise."

The house still took Poly's breath away. Everything seemed so nice, clean, and perfect with the huge windows looking over the ocean. The dual marble staircases wrapped around the stone area. A smaller stone path led downstairs. She remembered when they were on that very staircase and Joey hurt himself saving Julie.

His hand shook, as if she needed a reminder. He clinched his fist and shook his hand. She wrapped hers around it and gave him a smile.

"We have a problem on Earth we were hoping you could help us with," Joey addressed Jack.

"You've done so much for us, I don't think we can say no to anything you request."

"There's an illness spreading, a cough."

Jack's eyes went wide and he took a step back. "A cough, like *the* Cough? Is it killing people?"

"Yes, and Hank has it; only has a day left they said," Poly said choking up.

"And my mom."

Jack shook his head in disbelief, staring at his Panavice. "I don't . . . Harris is expected to be back any second." He talked into his Panavice and Harris appeared, kneeling next to the stone. His smile changed to a concerned frown as he took in their looks. "What's wrong?"

"Earth's got the Cough," Jack supplied.

Harris slid his hand down his face. "Jack, have Sanct check their vault for vaccines. If it's the same thing we dealt with, we may have a few stored."

"Can you make more?" Joey asked.

"We're barely managing to keep up with food production here, nor have we made a vaccine in hundreds of years. I'm afraid we aren't equipped to help much."

"He's dying." Poly's voice cracked. "Hank, he needs our help."

"I'll do everything I can." Harris held his Panavice to his face and then seemed to change his mind. "Maybe you should talk to Travis, you'd get a better response." He offered the Panavice to Poly.

Poly took the Panavice and pressed the call button.

"Yes," Travis's voice was filled with venom, he must have caller ID.

"This is Poly."

"*Poly*," his voice changed instantly. "How are you, is everything okay?"

She filled him in on the details and he said he'd check on it himself, immediately.

They waited an hour. Poly spent much of the time standing next to the glass windows, gazing down at the ocean feeling the guilt of being a possible carrier of the cough. The stone hummed and she whipped around. Joey held his gun out and Travis appeared, holding a black case.

"This is all we have." He rushed to Poly and handed her the case. "There might be a hundred in there."

Poly winced at the number. She needed a few billion. Now she would have to choose who lived and who died. She didn't want to play God, but she would if it meant curing those she loved. Extending her hand for the case, Travis pulled it back.

"I'm not giving it up until you promise to take the vaccine. It'd be just like you two to give it to everyone else but yourself."

"Fine," Poly huffed.

"It works as a cure as well," Travis said, handing it to her. "I wonder if one of you transmitted it to Earth. How else could it have gotten there?"

Poly hadn't thought about it that way. She looked down at the case and the back of her hand holding it. That hand could be transmitting stuff from world to world. Astronauts were quarantined when they came home from the moon, how was what they did any different? What they were doing was actually much worse, as people and grinners lived on the planets they visited.

She felt a tickle in her throat. She tried to push it down, but it forced itself out in a cough. The looks of fear spread across each of their faces. Were they scared for themselves, or for her?

"You feeling okay?" Joey asked and put his hand on her shoulder.

"Yeah, just got a bit of a dry throat."

"We better get you back to Earth." Travis ushered them to the stone. "How's Julie?"

"Good." There was something in his eyes, like he wanted to ask another question, but didn't. "Thank you for getting us what you could."

"We'll keep looking, there might be some stored elsewhere." Travis stepped out of the designated circle area.

"I will as well," Harris added from the edge of the circle. "But hurry, you need to get that to Hank and your mom."

Joey slammed in the code and the stone hummed.

"Come on," Poly said. With the cure in her hand, she felt an urgency building.

Jogging through the forest they got back to their car. Poly dropped the pedal to the floor on her way to the gym. Joey held on to the case with one hand and the grab bar with the other. She glanced at the case, trying to think of a plausible explanation of where she would get such a thing.

After a brief discussion, it was obvious they couldn't make a public announcement about having a cure, they would be trampled. So they decided to do it on the sly. They wouldn't tell anyone what they were doing.

Poly switched the headlights on as she pulled into town. Cars lined the road as she approached the gym. They'd only been gone a couple hours, yet the line had turned into a large mob. Hundreds now stood outside, some waving their arms, others were collapsed on the ground.

"Things are getting worse," she said, parking the car a ways down the road.

She got out and eyed the case in Joey's hand. In it, one vial gun and about a hundred vials. Each vial represented a saved life, but it also represented a choice. Who lived and who didn't. Would they be the only people left in the world after this? Would the rest of the world perish but the hundred they chose? If that was the case, should they save multiple family members, or spread it out to strangers with different bloodlines? Her head began to throb under the pressure and enormity of it all.

Joey took a step onto the sidewalk, but Poly stood in front of him. "I'm not doing anything until you take a shot," Poly said.

"I was going to tell you the same thing, but I don't need it. I feel fine. You are the one who coughed."

"You've been around your mom and I'm not going to be changing your bedpan in a few days, Joey Foust." She'd said it louder than she wanted but it worked, he looked hurt.

"Fine, but you first."

"No, I know you'll run off with it or something stupid after I've got mine." She coughed to drive home the urgency. Her throat started demanding another cough, but she suppressed it.

Placing a vial in the chrome metal gun, Poly shot it into Joey's shoulder. His hand shook as he placed the end of the gun on her arm. As soon as the vaccine was injected, guilt spread over her.

"We should save one for my mom."

"Agreed." Though it hurt to use the words. They were already playing God and it made her feel queasy.

Making their way through the mob of coughing and yelling people, she couldn't help but wonder if a civil place like Preston was starting to lose it, what were big cities with anonymous faces doing?

The place had filled the cots and now people lay on the floor, on the stage, sitting against walls, coughing. Poly spotted Trip hovering over Hank's body. They rushed to him, being delicate enough to avoid the people on the ground. One person grabbed Poly's leg and begged for help. She pulled her leg from him and apologized. She wanted to open the case and cure the man right there, but she needed to get to Hank first. If anyone knew they had a cure, the mob would turn into a full riot. She hated making the decision, but she pushed on to Hank.

Trip greeted them. "What are you doing here?" His voice cracked and he rubbed his nose.

Lucas and Julie pushed off the wall to join the group around Hank. Julie stared at the black case.

"How's Hank doing?" Joey asked.

"I think he's sleeping. Though, I can't get him to wake up." Trip rushed the last words out and took a deep breath.

Poly gripped Hank's hand and felt warmth. Breathing a sigh of relief, she knew they had made it in time. Stage three put the person into a coma state, where they slowly drowned as their lungs filled. She listened to Hank's wheezing. "We have a gift from Harris."

Trip's eyes brightened as he stared at the black case.

Poly opened the case on the floor and set a vial in the gun. She shot the vial into Hank's arm and placed another vial into it. She then shot it into the arm of Trip without asking.

"Hey," he protested.

"I know you would have said no."

"Dang right I would have. Look at the people around me. They need it."

"We don't have enough," Poly whispered trying to drive home the information.

Lucas walked over, pulling his sleeve up. "Hit me up with some of that." He cleared his throat. "I'm feeling it coming on." He did look a bit on the ill side, but he had ever since he'd been bitten by that grinner. The only person in all the worlds to be immune . . . did Lucas even understand how many lives he saved on Vanar?

Poly shot him in the arm and then did Julie as well. How selfish of her, she was glad to be saving the ones she loved, but it hurt her soul to let the rest die. The sounds of wheezing, coughing, moaning, and crying crashed into her. There were hundreds in the gym, hundreds outside. She shook her head. "I don't think I can do this."

"The president just announced he's shutting down all airports and putting the country in a state of emergency." Julie held her Panavice so they could see the headline on the screen.

Poly looked around the gym, thinking of how she would distribute the last of the cure.

"Please tell me you have more than this?" Julie asked, looking in the case.

"It's all they had," Joey answered.

"This is going to cause a riot," Julie said eyeing the people nearby.

"Do you know how much people would pay for this stuff?" Lucas said. "What? I was just joking." He rubbed his shoulder where Poly injected him.

"Do you have a cure?" A man next to Hank asked and then went into a coughing fit.

Poly felt the brick in her throat as she stared at the man. "It's just a cough suppressant." She hated lying, but she couldn't have the entire gym hog piling on them.

"We should leave here," Julie whispered. "If we can get this into the right hands, they can copy it and mass produce a cure."

"And where should we say we got this?" Poly asked.

"I don't know, maybe we can just mail it to the CDC or something."

"They'll find us and ask questions we can't answer. Like, what's that device you have, miss?" Poly pointed at Julie's Panavice.

"Guys," Hank sat up, "how did I get here?"

"Hank," they said in unison, rushing to his side.

"We found you on the road," Poly said. "You don't remember?"

"I remember leaving my house." Hank took a deep breath and then coughed. "Did they find a cure?"

"This one's better! They have a cure. Give it to me!" The man fell off his cot and went into a coughing fit, blood flung from his mouth as he did. The rustling of the man caused a stirring in everyone nearby.

"We better get out of here," Julie said.

"We can help them," Poly said. She pulled the case out and loaded a vial in the gun. She rushed over to the man on the floor. "This will make you better." She shot it into his arm.

"Please, help me." A woman, looking like a grinner stumbled forward and Poly shot her in the arm.

In less than a minute, Poly found herself in the middle of dozens of grabbing hands, coughing faces surrounding her like a horde of grinners. She reloaded the gun and fired into the nearest person, but someone else grabbed the gun and tried to shoot the empty vile into her own arm.

Joey moved next to her and pushed the person back, taking the vial gun from her hands. The crowd roared at this and pushed against them. "Get out of here," he yelled.

Poly brushed her hand over her dagger, but did not remove it from its sheath. She couldn't harm any of her own people, even if they wanted to rip them apart. Her small frame tried to push back and clear a space so she could reload the gun, but as she bent down to grab another vial, a person fell on her back, pushing her to the ground.

Her face slapped the smooth wood floor of the basketball court. She heard Joey screaming for her, but he sounded distant. A foot slammed against the back of her head and the pain was immediate. A knee jabbed her in the back and many hands scattered around her as they grabbed for the case and gun. Bare feet pushed against her face and she tried to move, but the weight of all the people pinned her down. Poly squeezed her body in and got away from the feet. She held the gun and case close to her chest and curled herself into a ball, trying to protect the remaining vials and her own vital body parts.

A woman pressed against her and coughed in her face while trying to pry Poly's hands free. More anonymous hands joined in as they assaulted her.

"Poly!" Joey yelled again.

"Joey," she tried to yell, but the sheer mass of bodies pushing against her wouldn't let the air escape. She tensed her body as tight as she could, trying to keep them from crushing her. The gym went dark with all the bodies piling over her. She couldn't breathe, and she knew if she didn't get up soon, she was going to die.

All she wanted to do was cure them.

CHAPTER 4

HELICOPTERS WERE LOUD, SO LOUD that Samantha had to wear noise canceling headphones to be able to communicate with the people sitting right next to her.

"Ten minutes 'til we're there, Miss Samantha."

Miss Samantha? It made her smile. Many people around the office had been calling her that lately. The smile faded as she gazed at the passing fields below. She was returning to her home town in a freaking helicopter. She should be excited to show everyone she'd made it in the big city; she didn't need the Six. But her nerves were creeping in, increasing every second they came closer to her old school.

She looked at the papers detailing the bodies and infected in the school gym. She scanned some of the names on the list and stopped cold at Hank. Her heart stuttered and tears welled in her eyes. Hank had never done her wrong. The guy had always been there when any of them needed him. Her heart went out to him and was even more thankful for what she was bringing to them all.

Preston was only the beginning. The whole world needed her.

The two helicopters flanking her on each side, carried enough of the cure to supply the entire town. If it worked like Zach said it would, the world would be clambering for it. She hadn't a clue how Zach had found a cure so fast, but she knew the man was the smartest person she had ever met.

"Five minutes, Miss Samantha."

"You know, you can just call me Samantha."

The man sitting next to her holding a machine gun nodded. She had grown used to guns working for Zach. Guards patrolled everywhere now and Zach personally saw to training many of them. And from the rumors spreading around the company, she gathered he could take on as many trainees as they could find. The man earned so much respect in such a short time, it was hard not to gravitate toward him.

A few houses passed under her and in the distance, the town's buildings popped in and out of sight as the trees obscured much of the town. She knew exactly where the school was and kept her eye on the growing building. Her heart pounded in her chest. *What if Joey and Poly are there?*

Taking a few relaxing breaths, Samantha counted in her head. It was something Zach had told her to do if she became nervous. She had no idea why he thought she should be the one to launch the cure, but she was glad to save her town, glad he picked Preston as an example to the rest of the world. It was curious he hadn't chosen his own hometown . . . but she couldn't waste too much thought on that as the helicopters hovered over the field next to the school.

All three lowered and the dust swirled around the windows. She felt the abrupt landing and watched as the three men with guns went out the door, fanning around outside.

Most of the country was starting to fall into chaos, so Samantha understood why the security was necessary. But it still felt weird having a group of armed men protecting her. She didn't feel as important as everyone treated her.

Adjusting the black suit Zach had made for her, she checked her hair and makeup in a small compact mirror. It had been done prior to arriving and she wished she felt as confident as she looked. The whole world would be watching this soon.

One of the armed men moved up to the helicopter door. "All clear, Miss Samantha."

"You're not going to stop with that, are you?"

"No, ma'am."

It looked like she was going to have to suck it up and get used to it. The man helped her down the small steps. Her black heels stepped onto the dirt and at once she felt a connection to Preston. The playground behind the school, the dirt track they ran miles on. She saw the window to Mrs. Nires class and looked away. *I'm not here for memories.* She was here to save her hometown and prove to the world Zach's cure worked. She knew it did already, they tested it on numerous people at headquarters, but the proof would be in the showing.

Samantha walked toward the podium her people were setting up. A few of the Preston folk had already started gathering and more were coming from around the school parking lot. She tried to maintain a confident walk just like her preppers taught her. Head up, shoulders back, she looked ahead, just hoping she didn't trip.

Keeping her eyes on the podium, she slowed her walk. The last thing she wanted was to stand by while they finished building it. Instead, she timed her walk just right and arrived at the edge of the parking lot just as they finished setting it up. A large background was now up and displaying the ZRB logo for the company.

Standing on the stool behind the podium, Samantha watched over the people gathering around. Two cameramen they'd brought along pointed their cameras on her. She swallowed and took in the faces gathering around. She didn't see any of the Six or their parents. In fact, it didn't seem like enough people for the arrival they had. She gazed down at the gym across the parking lot. A mob of people appeared to be storming into the gym.

"What's going on?" Samantha asked a lady standing near the podium.

"Oh, some fool started a rumor that they had a cure in there. Please." She rolled her eyes and crossed her arms. "Wait, don't I know you?"

"I don't think so."

"What ya'll doing here, dustin' up the place?" An agitated man asked.

"Yeah, and who's ZRB?" Another man said.

Gunfire sounded, two distinct shots from inside the gym. The armed men around her gripped their guns and spread out in formation between her and the crowd. They pushed back a few people. She felt the deep nerves coming back. If someone was in danger, or killing people, they needed to stop it. She stepped off the stool and strutted toward the gym, Hank was probably in there.

"We can't go into that mob, Miss Samantha." The man stood in front of her, shielding her and also stopping her from moving forward.

She walked around him.

"No," the man said and rushed back around to face her. "I am under strict orders to have you safely returned. If you think this isn't the place to receive the first package, we have another town assigned."

Samantha stopped. Zach had ordered them to protect her, it was sweet but unnecessary. She gritted her teeth and watched the mob around the gym flooding out. Even with only a handful of people still lurking around her podium, it didn't matter, it was as much for them as for the rest of the world. Once they heard what she was going to say, they'd be running to her.

She shuffled a few blank pieces of paper on the podium and stared at the cameras pointing at her. "I'm here to report great news. Through a vast amount of effort and research, ZRB has produced a miracle—a cure for the cough and a vaccine for the unaffected."

The crowd around her stirred in excitement.

"Then where is it? I've got a wife dying over here."

"We have it right here." Samantha pointed to the nurses exiting the helicopters. They each lugged a few cases behind them, moving closer to the parking lot. "These people will give you a shot that will cure the cough and prevent you from ever getting it again."

"Is this from ZRB? Who the hell are you? Is this from the government?"

"Yeah, how do we know you aren't poisoning us?" Another called out.

Samantha took in the faces, a few she recognized, they were scared and skeptical. Looking down at the podium, she breathed deep. She hadn't been prepared to take questions. Pulling the pin from the back of her hair, her locks fell down over her shoulders. The women in the front squinted at her, as if trying to solve a puzzle.

"I'm one of you, Preston. My name is Samantha Roslin and I lived over on Olive Street with my mom, Gretchen, not long ago."

The crowd looked confused, as if she was lying to them. Another gunshot sounded from the gym.

"We need to get going," her guard urged. Gripping his gun, he lifted it toward the sounds of the gunshots.

"Listen, we have a cure and it is here. There are enough shots for every resident of Preston. I've taken it; all of our people have. I've personally seen it cure an infected already."

"Why hasn't the president said they have a cure?"

"The president doesn't know yet. The government would want to study this cure, test it for months on rats before a limited release to a test city. The red tape might go on for months, but does your wife have months? Do your friends have months? We can't afford to wait for this cure. So we are giving it for free to the city of Preston as an example of its effects.

"We can't rely on the government to save us." Samantha gripped the edge of the podium and stared into the camera. "I have a message for the world. This cure is real, and it will be free to all citizens, courtesy of ZRB. If your government isn't providing it for you in the coming days, then they are not agreeing to our terms of delivery. ZRB is here to serve the world in a time of great need, please demand that your government allows you access to the cure."

She stepped off the podium with a thunderous cheer from the crowd. *Good, they finally believe me.* Too bad she wasn't sure about the last part. Hopefully her words wouldn't incite riots. She marched toward the helicopter.

"Samantha!"

She heard a familiar voice yelling from the crowd. Glancing over her shoulder, she saw Julie and Lucas being pushed back by her men. Good, they would get the cure. And she was sure Joey and Poly were close by—thank God she hadn't seen them. She couldn't stand one more glimpse of their perfect life.

Turning back around, she quickened her pace toward the helicopter, wanting to be away from Preston, from them all. Bringing the cure was her final interaction with the people of her past. She would be able to sleep knowing they were still alive, but she could finally move on with her future.

The helicopter left the Preston area and she felt the door closing on that part of her life. She didn't think she'd ever be back there again. She could fly her mom to San Francisco, maybe even buy her a place on the coast line. Zach had given her such a massive salary, she could afford to take care of her now.

It felt good to be in charge of her own destiny for once.

CHAPTER 5

JOEY PUSHED AGAINST THE MASSIVE pile of crazed humans. He lost all courtesy as fear for Poly's life pushed at his insides. His heart pounded as he yanked a man off the dog pile. If she got hurt . . . he didn't want to think of it.

He heard Julie and Lucas yelling, their words muddled with the surrounding noises. His sole focus was getting to Poly. He hauled back on the shoulder of another man to uncover her body curled on the floor next to her case. But as he pulled away each person, another replaced them like a swarm. A man standing over her stepped on the back of her head and another woman fell, jabbing her knee into Poly's back. She was in trouble and the urge to slow down time crashed into him. He forced it away. Sweat dripped from his head as he pulled his gun and raised it above his head.

Two shots blasted in quick succession, silencing the mob as people stared at his gun. The people around him cleared a path. "Get away from her!" Joey yelled, pointing his gun at the man hovering over Poly. The woman on Poly's back stumbled backward.

Joey rushed to Poly's side and put his hand on her shoulder. She winced and opened her eyes. Recognition of who he was lit her eyes and Joey helped her get to her feet with her free hand. Lucas, Trip, and Julie rushed to his side.

"You okay? You hurt?" Joey searched her body.

"I'm fine." She took a few deep breaths and said, "Maybe a couple bruises."

He felt his eyes twitch, the anger building at the people around him. He turned in a circle, taking them in. They all stared in his direction, glancing from him to his gun. Were they sizing up their chances? If they rushed him, what could he do?

"Let's get out of here," Poly said, holding the case in her hand.

Joey nodded to Lucas and wrapped his arm around her.

"Helicopters landed next to the school," a man yelled from the door.

Why are helicopters landing? Has the government finally come to help?

Joey pushed passed people toward the door, keeping his hand on the gun. He gave each person standing in his way the strongest look he could muster. It must have worked as each stepped aside, opening a tunnel of sorts toward the door. Sneers and grumbles went abound as they passed by the coughing crowd.

"I'm going to stay with Hank," Trip said and hurried back through the crowd.

"I hear you have a cure."

Joey turned and found Sheriff Pick standing at the door, pointing his gun at him. His uniform clung to his body like he'd jumped in a river, coughing into his free hand while maintaining his level gun.

"You just drop that gun, son, and hand me the case." Sheriff Pick coughed into his sleeve and used his gun to point at the case and the floor. A bit of blood dribbled down his chin.

Poly sneered. "Fine, take it." She set the case on the floor and kicked it.

"Poly, no, my mom." Joey watched the case slide across the polished wood floor and took a step toward it.

The sheriff fired a shot into the floor next to him. Joey jumped back and resisted every urge to shoot back—he wouldn't miss. The man yanked it off the floor. He brushed back his greasy hair with the gun still in his hand. He looked frantically at everyone around him as he backed toward the door, pointing his gun at the greedy looking people closing in. After a few deft steps, Sheriff Pick was out the door and gone.

Joey let out a long breath. He needed those cures to help his family. His mom was coughing like heck when he left his house. How did all this happen so fast?

With the case and the cure gone, the sick people found their way to their cots or loved ones, some just fell to the floor, giving up. He knew them, and the sight of his town in such trouble made him ill.

"Julie and I are going to check out these helicopters. Maybe there's help," Lucas said and took Julie by the hand as they left the building.

"You saved me back there, Joey Foust." Poly pointed to the area she was almost trampled.

"Did they hurt you?" He glared at the people around them.

"I'm okay," she said. "You weren't thinking of going all slow-mo, were you?"

"Thinking it? Yes. But I didn't, I made a promise I intend on keeping. Besides, I had other ways to stop my girl from getting trampled. And really, I thought at any second you'd get stabby and fight your way out of there. So really, I saved everyone else's life."

"Aren't you the hero?"

A man approached them, coughing in his hands. "Did you really have a cure?"

Poly shook her head. "Nah, just a cough suppressant. You should get back to your bed. Everyone should get back to their bed," she said it loud enough that her voice carried over the whole gym. People grumbled but mostly coughed.

"Come on, I have something to show you." Poly put her arm around his.

They walked outside and the fading daylight gave him a chance to see the red, swollen mark on her neck. She wasn't okay, they had hurt her. Anger built up and he stiffened, turning and glaring at the door. He wanted to march back into that death pit and put a few marks on their necks.

Poly yanked on his arm and pointed ahead.

Where is everyone going?

The mob was moving toward a large white backboard with a finely dressed woman standing in front of it. He squinted and pulled Poly toward her. "Is that—"

"Oh my God, it's Samantha," she confirmed.

The woman on stage pulled her hair down and even from across the school yard, he knew it was Samantha. What could she possibly be doing there? Did she land with those helicopters in the field?

He jogged closer and heard her words blasting through the speakers. The crowd was fifty people deep and he half thought of using his gun to clear a path. He apologized as they plowed through the crowd, the mass cheering and roaring around him. Through all the hands in the air, he spotted Samantha walking away from the platform, heading toward the helicopter.

"Samantha!" he called. She kept walking. "Samantha!"

She glanced over her shoulder, then turned back around and climbed into the helicopter with an armed man.

He pushed his way to the front of the crowd where a group of guards pushed back against the front row. Julie and Lucas stood at the front as well and yelled for Samantha, but she was long gone.

"Get off me, dude," Lucas said to one of the guards.

"Form an orderly line or you will not receive treatment. We have enough for everyone, so please be patient as we move as fast as we can."

"What are you talking about?" Poly asked.

Men with cameras hovered in the background, pointing their large lenses at the people of Preston. The cheers had slowed to a murmur, mixed with coughs. Men with machine guns made people behave, apparently. Julie and Lucas paired up next to Poly and him, as the crowd moved around them.

They huddled close in all the hubbub. "What the hell was that about?" Poly asked.

Julie furiously moved her fingers around on her Panavice. She never had it out in public so she must have felt it was important enough for the risk. "I'm guessing ZRB slash Marcus recruited her for this very reason."

A job fair had come to the high school last year and Samantha had been wooed by this ZRB company. Joey hadn't thought much about it, and Julie said they were a startup and probably wouldn't make it a year, but now they were landing helicopters and delivering a message?

"I don't care if they find me," Julie said, typing into her Panavice. "I'm going find out very quickly what this ZRB has turned into," Julie said.

"What was Samantha saying up there?" Joey asked.

"Dude, she was all primed and looking good," Lucas said. Julie nudged Lucas's shoulder. "She was going on about how the world could get their cure if they just called ZRB and requested it. Something about telling the people of the world if the governments didn't get it to them, it was because they wouldn't agree with Zach Baker's terms. Oh, and Preston was an example city or something for the cure."

Julie raised an appraising eyebrow at his lengthy synopsis.

"Did you guys see her look at me at the end there?" Lucas said. "I mean, she looked *straight* at me—she heard me—but she turned anyway, and went into her helicopter." He crossed his arms and huffed.

"She brought a cure?" Poly stared at the white tables, watching people getting injected in the shoulder at a rapid pace.

Joey couldn't believe what he was hearing. Even when Julie showed the information to him that ZRB was possibly Marcus, he didn't want to believe it; Samantha couldn't be fooled so easily. He hadn't seen or heard a thing from Samantha in a long time and now she lands in a helicopter and delivers something the whole world would go to war over. It seemed insane and he waited for the cameras to turn on him and for someone to come running out to tell him he was part of the biggest prank ever. He felt his heart in his throat. Marcus had Samantha. Was she being coerced into working for him? Was he torturing her?

"There's no way in hell I'm taking a cure from him," Lucas said.

"Some scumbag stole ours," Joey said.

"He didn't actually steal anything." Poly pulled her hand out of her pocket, holding a handful of the thin glass vials. She reached into her jacket and showed them the vial gun.

"You gathered all that up while they were trampling you?" He shook his head with admiration.

"Oh no, their servers..." Julie turned, showing her screen to them. Just a bunch of lines on a graph. "I'm not going to be able to hack into their servers anytime soon." Julie lowered her Panavice to her leg and blew air into her bangs.

Joey didn't care about the servers, he wanted to get Samantha out of there. She had never seen the videos of Marcus, he could be pulling her strings and she wouldn't even know. "We need to get her out of there, who knows what he's doing to her? Where's their headquarters? Where's she being held?"

"Just outside of San Francisco."

Joey turned and walked toward Poly's car.

"Wait!" Poly grabbed his arm and yanked him around. "We can't just go storming off to Marcus's house. He isn't like the others. We have to be a step ahead of him right now. You don't think he sent her here by coincidence? You don't think he knows we know now?"

"She's right," Julie said. "This is part of a plan." She shook her head and gazed at the remaining helicopters on the field. "This was the equivalent of leaving a business card with Marcus Malliden on it at our front door. Brazen, really."

"I say we go to this San Fran headquarters place and kick in the front door." Lucas kicked the air in demonstration of the kick he'd use.

"I'm with Lucas on this one." Joey finally agreed with him on something.

"Yeah, let's go all gangster on them. Maybe we can take him by the tie and pull him through the offices, show everyone up in there whose boss." Julie used her sarcastic gangster voice. "Bring our gats up in there."

"Now you're talking," Lucas said.

Julie took a deep breath and placed her hand on her forehead. "You're talking about the most dangerous person ever. A rank ten. A guy who could probably kill anyone on this planet. Have any of you seen his fight videos? And don't even get me started on the code written by that guy."

"Fine, what do *you* think we should do?" Lucas crossed his arms.

"We can't just leave her with that monster, I mean, look at what he's done already." Joey pointed to the coughing line of people.

Julie stared Joey in the eyes. "This is the harder part. We are nothing but a fun side note to him; a child's favorite play toy he brought to the park. We're nothing. He will have a much bigger game even than this." She pointed to the orderly lines forming.

"I like to think I'm something," Lucas said. "I did get a medal for archery."

"Regional medal in recurve bow," Julie corrected.

"Don't down play it, I'm *huge* in some circles."

Julie ignored Lucas and focused her attention on Joey and Poly. "If I had to guess, this Cough is about to get much worse before it gets better and when the world is begging for mercy, guess who has the cure?"

Joey's gaze went wide and he looked at the coughing people. It wasn't about making them suffer, it was about setting himself up to be the hero, to be the person the world was going to turn to . . . and he used Samantha to deliver the message. It finally sunk in. "He'll be expecting us," he said.

"Yep."

"What if we do the unexpected?"

"I'm all ears."

Joey laid out the idea, which started with getting their cure to their entire family; he didn't trust something that came from Marcus, or Zach, or whatever he wanted to call himself. Then, they'd get Samantha out of his foul hands and end his life at any cost. This would be the last time he allowed Marcus to control his life.

CHAPTER 6

THE NEXT MORNING AFTER HER trip to Preston, Samantha slammed her finger on the remote button and the TV clicked off. It was too depressing seeing the way people were suffering. Samantha felt the tears welling up in her eyes. She wanted to rush the cure out to the world and fix them. No one needed to suffer. Maybe she should visit the factory herself and see what the holdup was with the production line. They needed to make it faster.

Even as they bought four flu vaccine plants this week, it would take another few weeks to get the materials in to get them up and running. She made more calls and pushed more people than she thought was ever possible to speed it up. People's lives were in her hands now. She owed it to them.

She felt a hand glide over her shoulder. "You okay?" Zach asked.

"Yeah, just want to get this cure out to the world. Have you seen what's going on in LA?"

"Yes, it's tearing me apart. And from what I heard this morning, Mexico City is in total collapse."

"Zach," Samantha turned and gave him her best strong but stern face. "I don't think the world has a couple weeks, there might not be a couple *days*. We need to act now."

"I hate seeing you like this." He gave her the puppy dog eyes and adjusted his tie. She smiled and looked away, it was such a stupid look, but it still made her giddy every time. "What if I can get another city a cure? A major city. You choose." He sat on the edge of her desk.

"You have some ready to go?"

"I was leaving it as a surprise for you."

"You know I hate surprises."

"I know, that's why it's fun."

She felt heat flooding her stomach. Zach had started to make her feel things she thought she might never feel again. Just being in the room with him made the old feelings fade to black. Sucking in a breath, she held it. One city . . . how could she choose? "Do we have enough for LA?"

"Yes."

"I think we should do a highly populated city. New York doesn't seem as bad."

"Yet," Zach added.

"LA then."

"Done." He tapped his fingers on the desk.

"What else have you been keeping from me?" Samantha's coy smile spread across her face and she took a step closer to Zach.

He rose from the desk. "Did I tell you I like the color purple? It's like, my favorite color."

"I pegged you as a fan of blue."

"Mix in some red..."

"And you've got purple."

"Exactly." He moved closer to her.

The magnetic pull of him sucked her in. Samantha's hands shook and her heart beat fast. They were in her office, windows all around. Anyone could be watching them. Oh God, they'd all think she'd slept with the boss and that's why she got promoted to VP.

Who cares? Let them think what they want. She moved closer, taking a quick glance at those perfect lips before closing her eyes. She wanted to feel a connection again with a man. Maybe it would help her forget.

Two knocks sounded on her glass door. "Miss Samantha?" Her secretary, Ashley, stood there with a stack of papers in hand. "Sorry if I interrupted anything."

Samantha took a step back and felt part of Zach's favorite color heating her cheeks. She cleared her throat. What was wrong with her? It was her boss and he was older. How old though? She had to find out the exact age. Twenty-nine would be the cut off. Okay, maybe thirty. But that was *it.* Why wasn't he looking away? Why wouldn't Ashley get the heck out of the office?

Zach cleared his throat. "Why don't we finish discussing this later?"

"Sounds good. And I expect an immediate delivery of the promised . . . delivery." She winced at her stupid words. Ashley stood in the room looking as if she made a huge mistake entering.

"Of course. I'll see to it personally." Zach gave her a grin and left the room.

Samantha dropped into her chair and slid behind her desk. Her heart still raced and thoughts of Zach's lips floated around in her head. She breathed through her nose, trying to calm herself down.

Ashley approached the desk with a raised eyebrow. She was probably twenty-two and full of experience with men. She wouldn't be reacting this way if a man moved within inches of her. Ashley kept a smirk on her face and Samantha tried to stare it away.

"Just set them on my desk," Samantha said with a straight back. "I don't need any more reports for now."

"He's cute," Ashley said, hugging the papers against her chest. She obviously wasn't going to let it go.

Samantha pursed her lips and tried to find a way to diffuse the stupid look on Ashley's face, like she had a secret. A secret she could spread around the office, if she so chose. "I hadn't noticed."

"You were intimately close." Ashley placed the pile of papers on her desk. "It's not like the other girls around here haven't tried. Most thought he was gay or something." She sped up her words. "I mean, it's just that they've done almost everything to get his attention, yet he doesn't even look . . . I mean, they wear stuff. . . ."

"I think I get what you mean." Samantha found it fascinating that Zach didn't look at the other women. He'd always done the standard glance down with her. She didn't mind it, it was just something all men did, but if she was the only one he was doing it to, should she feel special?

"Let me know if you need anything else, Miss Samantha."

She hated the name at first and hated herself more for getting used to it. They just wouldn't stop saying it. Who started it anyway?

Ashley stood at the desk, rocking back and forth on her heels. Her strained face appeared as if she was struggling to keep back words.

"Is there something else?"

"I heard you picked a city. Can I know what it is? I mean, my family lives in the Napa Valley area. I was talking to my mom last night and she said Dad was starting to cough, she tries to tell me it's just a cold, but I can hear him coughing in the background. I know it's the Cough."

The Cough wasn't the scientific name, but slang Americans adopted. Kind of like Swine Flu, or Spanish Flu, the plagues often went by simple names everyone could follow. Samantha and the rest of ZRB had taken the vaccine, but it wasn't available for families yet.

She hated this part of the job. "I'm afraid I can't say."

"Please, Miss Samantha."

"If I send it to Napa Valley, will you call me Samantha?"

Her eyes went wide with fear, mouth opening and closing. Finally she nodded her head.

"The whole world will be getting cured as fast as we can make it. I'd tell your family to stay inside and avoid other people."

Ashley's features slumped, she knew when she was getting the shove off. She turned and left Samantha's office.

Samantha plopped her hand on the pile of papers and tapped her fingers. The papers were reports and estimates on production schedules. She could look at all the papers and search for inefficiencies, but it made more sense to go straight to the source. Zach seemingly had endless amounts of money, they could pay the factory workers to work double shifts for triple pay or something—anything to get the product out faster. She stood up and decided to take a field trip.

THE SPARSE ROADS HELD FEW cars and even fewer people. Some hugged the sidewalks, looking lost, while other staggered, coughing into their sleeves. One man lay on the edge of the road with his eyes open, staring at something in the distance. She knew him to be dead and stepped on the gas to get by him, keeping her attention straight forward. It made her think of Ryjack. The idea of Earth resembling anything like that horrifying planet terrified her. She kept a heavy foot and got there in under an hour.

She drove into the parking lot filled with cars. The cars looked uniformly parked and all had a thin layer of dust coating them, as if they were in a lazy man's car dealership. Maybe Zach was pushing the workers to the extreme. She admired the employee's dedication to stay at the factory for who knows how long.

Not finding a parking spot, she pulled next to the front door, adjacent to the sidewalk. The large single-story building looked like a distribution center; no windows and only a few truck doors lining one side. She left her car and walked to the front door. It had a closed sign on it. She tapped her knuckle on the glass and held her hand up to shield her eyes, trying to find movement inside. A man in all white walked to the door.

He spoke through the glass. "This is a restricted building."

"I'm the VP of ZRB, Samantha Roslin. I'm here to see Scott Fuller."

The man's eyes narrowed and he looked her up and down. "Stay here."

After a few minutes, she spotted another man with the first. He opened the door wide and smiled. "Samantha, what brings you here?"

"I wanted to check on production."

"I'm afraid that can't happen right now. There's been a leak and we had to shut down most of the building."

Samantha studied the man's face. Did he think she was stupid? "Are you Scott?"

"Yes."

"Then step aside and let me into my factory."

"I'm sorry but I can't allow that . . . protocol."

"Do you want to keep this job? Do you want to get a cure for your family, your town?" Samantha fought to get the words out. It felt wrong to say, but the look on his face said her threats were working.

"You wouldn't."

"Do you think Zach would listen to his VP or some factory worker?" She hated herself for talking to the man like that, but the world depended on getting the cure out as fast as possible. His feelings may have to get hurt.

"Fine, but you'll have to go to our quarantine room first. We can't have any foreign contaminants introduced." Scott led her into the building and past a metal detector and a machine that puffed air over her body. Then Scott took her to a small room near the detectors.

"We just need to have you in this room for a bit while the air scrubs you down."

"Is this really necessary?"

"I'm sorry, Samantha, but it is."

At least he wasn't calling her Miss Samantha. "Fine, but I want to discuss all the questions I've been emailing you."

"As soon as you're scrubbed down, we can sit at my desk and go over everything." Scott left the room and closed the door.

Samantha huffed and took in the room around her, a blank room with four walls and a door. The door contained the only window in the room. It faced the adjacent wall of the hallway. She'd expected some kind of machine to turn on, or puffs of air to shoot over her body. Maybe the ordinary fluorescent light on the ceiling was purifying the air around her?

After half an hour she began to be suspicious and pace.

An hour after that, she pounded on the locked door and yelled Scott's name. How dare they lock her up! She had turned from guest to prisoner and if she ever got out, she'd make sure they were all fired and criminally charged for imprisonment. They couldn't just hold her in a room like this. Didn't they know she was the Vice President of the company?

The bottoms of her hands hurt, but she slammed them against the door harder. No one came. In fact, no one had moved by the door since they left her in there. She was about to hit the door again when she heard a voice. Someone distant and angry—a person yelling. Relief then flooded her as she spotted her salvation.

Zach stomped to the door and flung it open. His face was red with anger and his normally perfect hair looked tossed and turned like he'd just toweled it from a shower. "Are you hurt?"

"No." She rushed into his chest and wrapped him in a hug. His arms pulled her in tighter, pushing some of the air from her. She held back tears and talked into his chest. "They imprisoned me. I want them fired."

"They thought they were doing the right thing. We've had . . . attempts to infiltrate our stocks. But you don't ever have to worry about Scott again. He's been taken care of." Zach spit out the words and wiped his hair back with his hand. "Let's get you out of here." He took her hand and led her down the hallway.

Even with the horribleness of being trapped in the room for over an hour, Zach's hand energized her. The skin on skin contact sent a warm sensation up her arm. She pulled him back. "Wait, I came here to check on production."

Zach stopped and turned to face her at the front door of the building. "We can't, there's been a chemical leak and they had to shut down for the day."

"But what about the cars—"

"I have a job for you, actually. I would love for you to cut the ribbon at the distribution of the cure in LA tomorrow. I have two-hundred trucks and teams set up, but I want you to launch truck one. The mayor will be there as well."

"That's great news. Are you coming with me?" She crossed her fingers.

"Sorry, I'd love to, but I'll be on international calls all day trying to get the cure distributed to other countries."

"Okay." She followed him to the parking lot and next to her car.

Zach grinned. "You want to travel in a bit more style?"

"What do you have in mind?"

A large black helicopter flew over their head and landed in the road. "One benefit of no one leaving their houses . . . open roads."

"What about my car?"

"I'll have someone grab it and bring it back. Leave the keys in it."

She bounced with excitement. She loved riding in the helicopter. Up in the sky, the world seemed normal again, she couldn't see people coughing or dead in the road. She frowned at the thoughts of distancing herself from it all.

Shaking it off, she reminded herself that tomorrow she would get to deliver the cure to a large population who needed it. Millions would be saved. She wouldn't be watching it from over a man's shoulder, or cowering at someone's feet. She'd be the hero this time. She hoped they would be watching.

Rushing to the helicopter, Zach held her hand the whole way. Once inside, Samantha gawked at the opulence. This one made her military grade helicopter look like a jerk. Cream leather couches, carpeted floor with white leather walls, and a ceiling with wood inlays. It felt huge inside with only a few seats.

"This is a bit nicer than the one I took to Preston."

Zach slammed the door and they got their seatbelts on. The room was quiet enough to talk with out headphones. "I'm glad you like it. I'll make sure to get you one."

Samantha laughed, sometimes he made the silliest comments. Like she would ever have a helicopter, let alone some fancy one. "Only if it comes with a white tiger to match the interior and I have to be able to hang my Lamborghini from the bottom. I don't want to arrive to a rental car."

"Of course, and let's make sure it's gold-plated with diamond ceilings."

"How about the floors?"

"Hundred dollar bills . . . they're so much plusher than twenties."

Samantha laughed and clapped. The helicopter lifted and she almost fell from her seat. Zach put his hand on her as the seat belt tightened around her waist. She laughed harder at her almost-fall and Zach joined in. Hearing him laugh made her heart beat faster.

The city view shrunk as the helicopter soared into the sky. The skyline of San Francisco appeared in the distance—such a beautiful city. Her heart sank thinking of its people suffering. "Zach, when are we going to go global with this cure?"

"Have I told you how glad I am to have you working with me?"

"Don't dodge the question."

"I'm not, I'm answering it." Zach took off his seatbelt and got closer. She held her breath as he took her hand in his. He'd become comfortable with casually touching her, and she didn't mind a bit. "This is just the start of creating a better world to live in. We cure this and something else will pop up, another problem, another war. As long as we're divided by borders and currency, the world will never see peace. I'm trying to use this horrible pandemic to bring the world together. One united society, a stronger world."

Samantha thought of all the wars and scandals she'd seen on the news. "But that will never happen. All these countries will never give up their borders."

"And they don't have to. I'm simply trying to get them to see that there should be a system in place for the whole world to follow—a single set of laws. We could end the wars. Don't you want that too?"

"Just seems like an impossibility."

"Normally, yes, but the Cough puts our foot in the door. Only at times of great suffering is there potential for great unity."

Samantha loved his vision of the world. How could such a young man have such ambitions? If only the world would come together and fight a common enemy like the Cough. "And who would rule this new world?" she asked.

"I would of course." He smiled and raised an eyebrow. "You can rule as my Vice President."

"Okay, I'll take Switzerland."

"How about all of Europe? I'll take the Americas."

Samantha enjoyed the easy, playful banter. It kept her mind from racing to the horrors surrounding her. The Cough, the Preston Six, Joey and Poly . . . every moment she spent with Zach, she left a bit of her old life behind and looked forward to this new life. "Can I ask you a question?"

"Of course."

"How old are you?"

He laughed again. A soft laugh, pleasing to the ears. "How old do you think I am?"

She wanted to find out more about Zach and what made him laugh. "Mid-twenties?"

"I'm twenty-seven."

He barely made her cut off at eight years her senior. Not that it would have mattered what his age was, she felt an attraction to the man, not the years behind him. She scooted closer to Zach squeezing his hand and pulling him a bit closer to her face, intent on finishing what they started in her office.

"Sir, we have a problem at headquarters," a voice warbled out from speakers above them. "There appears to be an attack in progress."

Zach bounded to the window and gazed below.

Samantha rushed to her window and looked down to find a small group of men dressed in black, moving across the parking lot with a large armored vehicle as cover. Each of the men carried a rifle and marched toward the front doors. She looked for markings on their clothes but there weren't any. If it wasn't the police or the military, who could be attacking them?

Zach pushed a button on the wall and spoke into a speaker. "Land us behind them."

"Yes, sir."

He took on the dangerous vibe Samantha had seen before. She split her attention to the men rushing for the front door of their headquarters and Zach's fiery looks. He noticed her staring.

"Don't worry, this helicopter is bullet resistant."

Her heart pounded in her chest. "Resistant?"

"There's only a dozen of them. I won't let them hurt you or anyone else." He kept his eyes on his targets as they descended. "Stay in the copter, okay?"

"Yeah." She had no intention of getting into a shoot-out with those thugs. Zach knew there would be people willing to kill for what they had and he'd set up many security measures to deal with them over the last few weeks. It didn't make her afraid of the situation any less though. She winced when the helicopter touched the ground.

Zach tossed his jacket to the floor and stuffed his large tie clip on his belt before tossing his tie to the floor. He lifted the bench seat, revealing a cache of weapons. He glanced at her and raised an eyebrow. A dozen men were trying to take down ZRB and Zach looked amused. He pulled out a couple handguns and a machine gun from the compartment. With the guns around him, he opened the door. Dust and bits of grass stirred up as he jumped out and slammed the door behind him.

Samantha pressed her face against the glass, watching as he ran to the parking lot full of armed men. It was either nuts or guts. Maybe a bit of both. The armed men watched Zach's approach. It wasn't as if he was trying to be stealthy . . . landing in a helicopter and all.

The men fired at him, bullets shattering the windows of the car he now stood behind. Samantha put a hand on the window and called his name, thinking Zach had been shot. He never even ducked behind the car for protection. Raising his gun, he then fired into the group advancing. They fell with each of his shots. She gasped at the brutality. Zach had just killed half a dozen men before the remaining few dropped for cover next to their armored vehicle.

She drew in a breath as the sounds of bullets ceased. At any second, one of those men could get a shot off on him. If Samantha had known he was going to be so reckless, she'd have forced him to stay in the helicopter and let the building security team deal with it. Who did he think he was, Rambo?

Zach moved forward, weaving in and around cars, flanking their position. He fired his handgun periodically, pinning them down. She squinted as he moved too far away from her to see clearly. She heard more gunshots and saw Zach standing on a car, firing down.

Samantha covered her mouth, terrified and thrilled at the same time. She'd seen Joey kill for her. She'd also seen Lucas kill those foul grinner things many times, even Poly had killed a fair share of them. But she'd never seen such efficiency, such fearlessness in any person. Where had he learned all this? The man knew everything, *had* everything.

He even has eyes for me. She put a hand on her chest and felt her heart pounding against her flesh. Her stomach felt warm and for some reason, she flushed—feeling stupid and excited at the same time.

Zach climbed onto the hood of the moving armored vehicle and shot into the windshield. It was so brutal, so exciting. His machine gun showered bullets into the protected windshield as it drove forward and crashed into another car. Zach fell backward onto the hood of the car it crashed into. He jumped to his feet like a lion and pointed his gun at various targets around the vehicle. He lowered the gun and then faced the building, motioning for people to come out. Giving a thumbs up, it must have been over already.

Many faces appeared in the windows of the building. Had they all been watching? He jumped off the car and made his way toward the helicopter. Samantha didn't blink, watching him cross the grass, strutting toward her. In the midst of the fire fight, his shirt had ripped open and she gawked at his chiseled body. She'd felt his fit form in a few lingering hugs, but it was better than she'd fantasized about. She wanted him, all of him.

Pushing open the door, she hopped out and jogged to Zach, keeping a hand on her swirling hair. Her heels stuck into the grass and she stepped out of them, not wanting anything to impede her progress. His smile took her in and she didn't need any words. Wrapping her arms around his neck, she kissed him.

Initially, the force of her body knocked him back, and then he firmed up like a piece of marble, holding her steady. His lips moved on hers and she felt his experience take over, kissing her deep and passionate. She felt weak as his hands moved down her back and his tongue parted her lips. The entire building had to be looking on from the windows.

They pulled away for a breath and Zach gazed into her eyes. "Took you long enough."

Samantha leaned her head back and laughed. She couldn't believe it was possible to find another man who made her feel the way Joey had. Best of all, it wasn't with some wishy-washy child of a man. He was a real man, who wanted her and no one else.

CHAPTER 7

JOEY AWOKE WITH A STIFF neck. Rubbing his eyes, he yawned. The car clock read *1:32am.* Turning to look at the backseat, he found Julie and Lucas sleeping, leaning on one another. Facing forward, his eyes met Poly's and she gave him a quick smile before turning her eyes back on the road. He loved waking up next to her and if she wasn't driving a car, he'd lean over and give her a few diversions. For now, he settled on grabbing her hand and resting them on the center console.

Taking advantage of her distraction, Joey let his eyes travel down her body at a leisurely pace. She wore a tight pink sweater that was formed to her figure, giving him a better view than what was outside the car. And for those few seconds, he didn't think about the Cough.

At least in the dark night he couldn't see the abandoned cars on the road, the closed up businesses, and worst of all, the walking Coughers. They staggered down the road, terrifying anyone nearby, like dark-aged lepers. It sickened him to see his world turning into a Ryjack. He'd do everything in his power to stop Marcus from killing off Earth. He'd also kill Marcus for taking Samantha once again.

Poly turned her head and smiled, but it didn't meet her eyes as she gripped the steering wheel and took quick glances out her window. "What does this place remind you of?" The headlights shone on a family walking down the road. One of the children raised a hand as if trying to answer a question in class. Poly glanced at the kid but didn't slow down.

"You think this is what Ryjack was like at the start?" Joey asked.

"If these people turn into grinners, I'm running them all over." She smiled and this time it felt genuine.

"There are worse things than grinners."

"Yeah," Poly said. "You actually think this Zach Baker guy is Marcus? I mean, how could Samantha be fooled?"

"I don't know, Julie seems confident, but Travis wasn't quite sold on the idea."

"I'm scared of what we're getting into."

"The great and mighty Poly is scared? Say it ain't so," Joey teased.

She rolled her eyes and glared at him with some humor in her expression. "I'm scared for different reasons than you think." She rubbed her thumb over the back of his hand. "You remember on the roof, right before Max took you?"

That moment on the roof was one of the best and worst times of his life. "Not something I could ever forget. Did I ever tell you I slowed time just to spend a little longer with you?"

She felt her cheek and shook her head. "You didn't have to, I already knew. Did you know that was when . . .?"

"What?"

"That was when I knew I could never live without you," she rushed the words out. "In less time than it took to blink my eyes, your lips touched my cheek and my world was forever changed." She faced him for longer than might have been safe, tears welling in her eyes. "I can't lose you again, Joey. I will die."

His heart fell and he rubbed the back of her neck, leaning across to kiss her on the cheek. "I won't let them take me or anyone else again. I promise." Even as he said it, he pictured Samantha. They had her.

"We're getting low on gas. There's a station up here." Her voice seemed shaky and he wanted nothing more than to show her how much she meant to him.

The gas station was selling gas for the reasonable price of twenty dollars a gallon, with a large handwritten sign that said *Cash Only*.

Joey waited for the car to come to a complete stop, then jumped over the center console to straddle Poly. She welcomed him, sliding her hands under his shirt, scratching light circles up and down his back. He tangled his hands into her hair and pulled her into a deep kiss. Adjusting his position, he angled his body so that her chest rubbed against his. Pulling the collar of her sweater to the side, he dipped his head down and ran his tongue along her collarbone.

She moaned and grabbed the back of his head. Joey pulled more of her sweater down and adjusted it to give himself better access, when his butt bumped the horn. Freezing, he looked up to a smiling Lucas.

"Please, by all means proceed. I love waking up to a live porno."

Poly yanked her sweater up and Joey retreated back to his side of the car. He took a deep breath and looked at the store. Clearing his throat, he wiped his mouth. "How much money we got left?"

"About five hundred," Poly said, looking into her small purse.

"Give me a couple hundred."

Poly handed him a stack of twenties. "I'm coming in."

"No, just get," Joey looked out the window at the pump number, "pump seven going. I don't want to spend any more time here than needed." He left the car and crossed the parking lot.

A few cars were parked at the pumps, but he didn't see anyone in them. In the darkness next to the station, he spotted a few more vehicles. They were all crooked, like someone skidded out as they parked. Or maybe they were shoved there, three deep.

Through the glass windows, Joey spotted a man standing behind the counter. He pushed open the glass door and a bell dinged. The man behind the counter looked sweaty and gave Joey a wave with a smile.

"Hey, just looking to get a couple hundred on seven," Joey said as he approached the counter. The entire place had been cleaned out, every shelf and every fridge. It sent chills down his back, thinking how similar it felt to the little mart Ferrell ran.

The man behind the counter wore a large green jacket with dark stains scattered on his undershirt. He rubbed his hand over his greasy hair and gave a nervous nod. Joey didn't feel right, something was missing from this puzzle. Where was everyone?

Joey placed the stack of twenties on the counter, freezing for a split second in shock. He didn't think the man caught his reaction so he kept his body language as casual as he could; trying not to look at the dead man who lay in his own pool of blood behind the counter.

"Got any supplies?" The man blurted out.

"Nah, we barely made it here."

The man twitched and glanced out at the car. His eyes lingered on Poly standing next to the pump. "Pump seven?"

"Yeah."

The man took the money and stuffed it in his pocket. "I'll kick it on for ya." He kept his eyes on Poly as he spoke. The man kept one of his hands under the counter the entire time.

Joey took a step back, keeping his attention on the man and his hidden hand. He felt the two guns under his jacket with his arms. His hands were shaky, but still fast if needed. He didn't want to kill the man though. He didn't want to ever kill another person.

Joey stepped back again and opened his jacket up, revealing his guns. The man began taking his hand out from under the counter and turned his attention back to him. "Listen, I just want to leave with my friends," Joey said.

The words stopped the man's hand from moving. "I can't let you do that."

"You don't have a choice." Joey slowed his breathing and felt the situation escalating. He readied himself to do something he'd promised he'd never do again. "Don't do this, you won't win."

"*Please*. Like some little piss-ant punk..."

Joey spotted the movement he was hoping wouldn't happen. In a split second, the quiet gas station at the end of the world ignited in a crack of a gun. The man fell, disappearing behind the counter. With two dead, Joey breathed out and looked at the end of his gun, questioning what he'd done. There had to have been a better way. Anger flooded him at how stupid the man was for making him do that. Why did he have to pull a gun on him?

A crashing noise from the back of the store sounded and a door busted open, revealing a man struggling to get his pants on. He dripped in sweat and had a stupid smile on his face. "You get another? I'm finished with the last one." The man's smile ended once his gaze landed on the end of a gun.

Joey felt rage explode as he thought of the putrid words spewing from the fat, disgusting man's mouth. What was he finished with back there with his pants off? Joey's mouth twitched and his hand shook. He tapped his finger on the trigger. The man wasn't armed, but how could he leave such a person alive?

"Please, kid. Don't kill me." The fat man fell to his knees, pants around his thighs, his white briefs clinging to his frame.

"What'd you do back there?"

The man's face went white and he jerked his attention from the open door to Joey. A new fear spread over his face. "I didn't do nothin'. It was Nate! He forced 'em back there. I just wanted to keep 'em safe."

The door dinged and Joey pulled his second gun out while keeping the first one trained on the fat man. Poly had a handful of knives as she scanned the room.

"I think it's just him," Joey said. "Don't you dare look at her!" He yelled as the fat man turned his attention to Poly.

"I wasn't looking, kid." The man slumped and looked at the white linoleum floor.

"What's going on?" Poly whispered.

"The guy behind the counter pulled a gun on me."

The fat man's face perked up and looked at Joey's chest. "Nate ain't got no gun. That guy behind the counter was dead when we got here. Someone shot him."

"Keep an eye on him." Joey walked to the counter and leaned over it, looking at the man he shot. He held a bottle of Jack Daniels in his dead right hand, some of the liquid had spilled out next to him.

He staggered back from the counter. *That* had been the familiar smell. Same stuff Trip drank. He felt like he was going to pass out. He'd done it again—killed a defenseless person. Unitas's laugh echoed in his head . . . he'd killed her as well, cold and heartless. The greasy man behind the counter was reaching for a drink, the sweats and weird way about him was because he was drunk. He had spent a year convincing himself he wasn't a monster, he convinced himself that he was worthy of someone like Poly. He wasn't righteous, he was stupid and reckless.

"You okay?" Poly asked.

"I shot him." He felt the blood draining from his face and he struggled to keep his hands on his guns.

"You ain't got to shoot another, kid. I'll go on and be out of here in two seconds, if that's what you want."

The words seemed distant as Joey struggled to walk toward the man. He needed to see what was hidden by the door, in the darkness behind. With each staggering step the fat man became more frantic in his motions, switching between Joey and the door.

"You don't need to look back there, kid. You don't want to do that," the man pleaded. He sucked in snot and held his hands together like in prayer. "Just get in that car and move on. You don't need to see what Nate did."

Joey did. He had to see it. He needed a justification for what he did or he'd never be able to move on from it. "Move away," he said with force.

The fat man scuttled back on his knees, belt buckle dragging on the ground. "I've got a few supplies in my car, you're welcome to whatever. Please, I don't want to die," the man's blubbering face squealed and it made Joey sick.

He stepped into the dark doorway, the back room, probably used as a storage room before the Cough. His hand slid on the wall and flipped the switch up, turning the light onto an utter nightmare.

His mouth opened in horror as his eyes popped from a woman's dismembered leg and body, to another young girl's carcass nearby. Several more were scattered around the room, without clothes, without dignity, and without a breath left in their battered and bloodied bodies.

There were a few more horrendous things within sight, but he refused to allow them to enter his conscious mind. Joey stumbled back from the doorway. His feet shifted in shock and he fell to his back on the white flooring. The fat man saw an opportunity and lunged for him.

Paralyzed from what he'd seen, Joey only had time to brace himself for the impact of the large man's body. Then he heard a thump. The man squealed out one last breath before collapsing on top of Joey's legs, a knife stuck into the side of his head.

He pushed the body off and scurried backward on his hands and heels. Sufficiently far away from the room and the fat man, he stopped. Still sitting on his butt, he pulled his knees up and buried his face into them.

Poly's hand rubbed his back.

The doorbell dinged. "What the hell?"

Joey didn't need to look up to recognize Lucas's voice.

"What was in the room?" Poly asked gently.

New fear washed over him and he sprung to his feet and ran to the door. He glimpsed the woman's dead foot and slammed the door closed. None of his friends needed to see what was in there. He no longer felt bad about shooting Nate. Now, he just wanted to shock his body back to life so he could kill him again. These nasty men needed to suffer for what they'd done. Joey paced in front of the door, feeling as if he might explode with anger.

Was this the new world? This was worse than any Ryjack or Vanar invasion. This was in his own backyard, a few towns over from Preston. This shouldn't be possible. Where were the cops? He thought of the Preston cop robbing them and it stung to think of a new reality on earth. Was man destined to become monsters? How could he let Poly live in such a world?

"I think I can get the pump going." Julie walked next to the counter, averting her eyes from the two bodies on the ground.

"What's up with that room?" Lucas asked, watching Joey pace back and forth.

"Don't ever ask me that again," Joey bit out, rougher than he wanted, but he was filled with such anger, anything he said would be rough.

Poly winced at his tone and they all averted their attention elsewhere. Good, he didn't want them seeing him, he didn't want to see himself. He wanted to jump into a body and mind that hadn't seen the things he'd seen, or done the things he'd done; anything to wash away the memories. What a cruel thing memory was, keeping the worst in high definition.

Julie got the pump going and they filled the car up. Poly and Joey took the back seat, while Julie drove and Lucas sat front passenger. Joey hadn't said a word since his explosion at Lucas. Only a few words had been shared between any of them.

"You two should get some sleep so you can take over in the morning," Julie said.

Poly touched his hand and he jerked it back. Quickly realizing his mistake, he reached for her hand and took it in his. It felt good to have her touch. He realized he hadn't thanked her yet. "Thank you for saving me back there."

"I couldn't let that disgusting man touch you."

Joey sighed and thought about the place they were going. It was heavily populated. If the outskirts and back roads hid these kinds of horrors, what would a big city entail? He only hoped they could get to Samantha before she found herself stuffed in the back storage room of a gas station. "Can we go faster?"

CHAPTER 8

SAMANTHA SKIPPED PAST THE OFFICES on her floor. She didn't care about what the others thought anymore. Nothing mattered at the moment, because she had Zach. The kiss they'd shared, the feeling of his body against hers, lifted her thoughts above the hate.

She bounced to her desk and plopped on her black leather chair. Pushing her feet against the floor, she glided to the window. She imagined what it had looked like from up there. Two people running across the grass field below, finding each other in an embrace. It was better than any book she'd ever read, and she got to live it. Once they cured the world, they could get on with their lives together.

Her phone dinged. It was Zach.

Zach: Missing you.
Samantha: When are you coming back?
Zach: A few days, it's bad out here. Stay there.
Samantha: Be careful.
Zach: I will.

She kicked off the window and wheeled her chair back to her desk, just as Ashley tapped on the glass door. She motioned for her to come in.

"Good morning, Miss Samantha." She wore a big frown.

Samantha wanted to smack it from her face. "Good morning, Ashley."

"I've got the itinerary set up for LA today."

That's what the frown was about. Ashley found out they wouldn't be saving her home town on the outskirts of San Francisco. Samantha didn't like choosing a city, but saving one of the biggest cities in the world seemed a good start. She could handle the domestic end of things while Zach talked to world leaders about international distribution. "Thank you, Ashley."

Ashley tapped on the desk and loitered.

Samantha huffed, leaning back and crossing her arms. "Go on, get it out." She probably wanted to gossip about her kiss or something.

"I know you and Zach have a thing.. . ." *Here we go,* Samantha sighed. "But don't you think he took on a bit much here? If we can get this cure distributed to the government, they could help us produce it. They have the man power to see it carried out. I mean the whole world is at stake here."

Samantha leaned forward and put her elbows on her wooden desk. Things were bad, but they were going to save them. They were going to save everyone. She would get to be the hero this time, not some cowered weakling standing behind five mighty warriors.

Narrowing her eyes, she looked at Ashley. This wasn't like her at all. She stood from her desk. Something was behind those words, or more importantly, someone. "Have you been contacted?"

Ashley rushed closer and placed her hand on the desk. "They want us to turn over all the data we have on the cure—they can help us. They said they can cure everyone, they just want to help."

"Who's *they*?" Samantha spit out. She didn't want someone to swoop in and steal what Zach had created.

"The president himself, Samantha, they called me—*he* called me. But I can't do it on my own, I need someone with the clearance to get through the blocks."

"Someone like me?"

"I know we haven't been the best of friends, but this is about more than just us. This is about the world. Just look at the news, listen to the radio . . . the Cough is destroying us and we have a cure. We have a cure that we can't make fast enough. We need help."

Samantha felt her painted nails digging into her palm. Ever since she'd made the announcement in Preston, the whole world wanted to take it from them. How foolish could Ashley be? "Did you see the president? Did he give you proof?"

A hint of doubt hit Ashley's face. "No, but I know his voice."

"A voice can be copied." There had to be more to it. "What did they offer you?"

"Nothing, I just don't think we should be holding this cure back from the world when they so desperately need it. My own mother is in stage three, Samantha."

She took out her phone. It didn't have a normal operating system. Actually, nothing was normal about it. Zach had given it to her on the first day she started work, confiscating her old phone for security reasons. It worked like any other phone, but there were a few buttons on it in case of situations like this one with Ashley. It gave her no pleasure to press it, she actually felt sad for Ashley.

"The cure is being created as fast as anyone can make it. Zach has purchased almost every vaccine factory in the country. How do you think the 'president,'" she used air quotes and rolled her eyes, "can do more than us?"

"It's not just that. Zach's doing stuff, Samantha, he keeps it from you," she whispered and stepped closer. "There are rules with you."

"What are you talking about?"

"You don't find it weird we all call you Miss Samantha? And that's just the start of it. We aren't allowed to be friendly with you. He tells all the women on this floor how to treat you."

Samantha shook her head in disbelief. It was the stupidest thing she'd ever heard and she'd hung around Lucas for most of her life. Why would Zach tell people to be mean to her? Why would he have them shove their smug noses in the air when she walked by? Samantha had learned, if things don't make sense, they're probably a lie.

She felt washed in lies growing up, but now she felt it anew, and Ashley was trying to steal it from her. She had to be jealous. She's the one who said all the women wanted Zach; she was probably one of them. "I don't believe you."

Ashley laughed. "You're drowning in infatuation, *Miss* Samantha. You can't see straight, you can't see what's in front of you."

Samantha stood from her desk and pointed at Ashley. "You don't know anything."

"This isn't high school anymore, *Miss* Samantha. You're playing with people's lives now, and it has to stop. We have to stop it. Now please, help me get the President of the United States that cure."

The door flung open. Five men, dressed in all black, flooded into the room and grabbed Ashley. Her face went pale and she flung around in their tight grip. "Samantha, no. Don't do this. This isn't right. You're going to kill us all!"

"*Wrong*," Samantha screamed. "All of this . . . simply because we didn't choose your city? No, you are the one who wanted to kill people. Your hometown has ten thousand people and today I'm going to save ten million."

"He's not who you think he is. He's lying to you. He's lying to all of us!" The guards pulled her flailing body out the door. She screamed more things as they hauled her beyond visibility.

Samantha, out of breath, placed both palms on the warm wood desk and leaned on it for support. Her heart raced and the anger slowly evaporated. Ashley planted a seed deep inside, and she wanted to get it out. She wanted to smack her for putting it there, a hint of doubt. Sure, some of the stuff Zach did didn't make sense, but the man had a greater plan, he wanted to change the world.

Her phone dinged with a text. She brought it up and saw Zach's text of concern. She replied with a quick version of what Ashley had done.

Samantha: Where are you?

Zach: About to meet with a prime minister of some tiny country in Eastern Europe.

Samantha: Are they signing the agreement?

Zach: I will guarantee it. I can hear his cough through the door.

Samantha: Good luck. I miss you.

Zach: Miss you too. I'll be home soon.

Samantha lay the phone on her lap and looked out the window. She almost wanted to be hopping around the globe with Zach, gathering signatures from the world's leaders. She couldn't imagine any country not signing the agreement, but Zach said he hadn't gotten a single response from the United States yet.

Another tap on her door.

Marge stood on the other side of the glass. She was an assistant to the human resources manager. Samantha shoved off the window and hoped for a better second conversation of the day. She motioned for her to come in.

Marge opened the door and fidgeted with her hands, looking nervous.

"Yes?" Samantha raised an eyebrow.

"I've been assigned as your new assistant, Miss Samantha." Marge seemed to want to be anything but that.

Samantha sighed. She would have to deal because she needed the help. She had an entire city to save, and then the world.

CHAPTER 9

"THIS IS THE THIRD HOUSE today," Trip said putting a finger through the bullet hole in the door. "I bet she didn't even see it coming."

Hank didn't want to look at the dead body just past the front door. He'd seen enough death and didn't need any more ghosts. His dad lingered at the door, looking in and then out.

"They're being shot as they answer the door," Trip said.

"We'll get these guys," Hank said.

"We better get to Gretchen's. Their trail is leading that way."

They got into Trip's truck and headed down the dirt road. Hank eyed the road and the surrounding fields. He picked up the radio and pushed the talk button. "Rick, how's it going on your side?"

"It's quiet, over."

"All right, we're heading to Gretchen's, over."

"Ten-four, over."

Hank wanted to call Joey and the rest of his friends, but the power was out and cell coverage was down. He sensed they were okay, but it would have been nice if he knew for sure. Just thinking of Samantha being near Marcus sent chills down his spine.

Gretchen's house appeared untouched as they pulled into the driveway. They still rushed to the door, looking for that signature bullet hole, but it was clear. Not sure if Gretchen would even get up to answer, Trip took out a key to unlock the front door.

"Gretchen," Trip called out as he entered the house, "it's Trip and Hank."

"Back here," she answered.

They walked past the family room, straight to the back bedroom. It used to be the guest room, but Gretchen had moved into it because stairs had become too difficult.

"Who's looking better today?" Trip said, taking a seat at the end of the bed.

Gretchen sat up and coughed into a handkerchief. "I'm feeling better. I was at death's door for a minute there. I thought I heard David calling to me." She laughed and then coughed again.

"Say, there's some men roaming around Preston, nasty men, killing people in a search for the cure." Trip looked at Hank and then back to Gretchen.

"Well, if I had some, I'd give it to them. Did you see what's going on out there? Pure chaos."

Hank nodded and thought about his recent journey through town. Ever since the world wide announcement that Preston had been given the cure, an onslaught of people had come into the town in search of it. At first, it was mostly friendly interactions with people full of hope, and when they realized there wasn't a cure for them, they left. Those were the good people. The bad and skeptical people stayed and demanded they deliver the cure, but those weren't even the worst.

The worst were the roaming bands of opportunists. They wanted the cure because they knew how valuable it would be to the right people. Or maybe they already worked for the right people. Either way, they were on a mission, methodically tearing apart an already fragile Preston.

"Why don't you get some sleep? We'll watch over the house for a bit—"

A knock sounded on the front door. Trip glanced at Hank and nodded his head. Hank left the bedroom and darted to the left side of the family room. He tried to see any shadows behind the pulled curtains but none appeared.

Trip flanked to the right and eased his way to the side of the door. He brought his handgun up to his hip. "Who is it?"

No answer.

Hank got closer to the front door and held out his gun, waiting for the signal from his dad.

"Anyone out there?" Trip asked.

"Sir, we are here to turn back on the power. We just need you to sign this release paper first."

"That would be the best thing ever. Let me unlock the door. Just a sec." Trip pulled an umbrella off the coat rack and poked the door handle, rattling it.

A gunshot blasted a hole through the door and struck the umbrella, sending it to the floor. Hank jumped back and nearly dropped his gun. Trip pulled out a fake groan of agony and pushed over the coat rack. It crashed to the floor. He held his gun out, waiting for the door to open. The man on the other side kicked at the door and then rattled the handle. He kicked again, but the door held.

"Need a breach here."

"Hank," Trip whispered, "get back and shoot the first person who comes through the door."

"What?" Hank heard him but couldn't believe it. He didn't want to kill these people. The gun shook in his hands.

They slammed something into the door and the jamb cracked.

"Wait!" Hank said.

"Hold," a man ordered.

"Dang it, Hank," Trip muttered.

"Listen, we don't want any trouble with you guys," Hank said. "We can end this amicably. You guys just leave Preston and we won't follow. No harm, no foul."

They laughed outside. "You give us your cures and we'll be on our merry way." They laughed again.

"If I give it to you, you'll leave Preston for good?"

"And never look back."

"Fine, but don't shoot. It's kept in a glass vial. One wrong move and I'll break it."

Silence, and the man's whimsy was gone. "You have it?"

"Yes." Hank opened his jacket and pulled out the vial. Poly gave them a few extra to make sure they had backups.

"Open this door and I promise, we won't hurt you."

"Don't do it, Hank," Trip said.

Hank walked to the front door, daylight streaked through the hole they made with the intention of killing his dad. He turned the handle and swung it open.

Four men stood on the front patio. Each held a gun and they were all pointed at Hank. He looked at them and their clean clothes and tucked in shirts. And the lead man with a mustache had an interesting pin on his shirt, a pair of triangles with a circle between them. It seemed out of place among all the earth tones he wore.

The man with a mustache extended his hand and held his other one back, holding his gun. "Okay, just hand it over, real slow."

Hank reached out the door and the man plucked it from Hank's grasp. The man gazed at it and held it to the sun. He smiled and showed the rest of the group. Hank slammed the door and locked it.

"Woo! Hell yeah. You got any more?" The man asked through the door.

"That's all of it," Hank said and started backing away from the door.

"Oh no, this is not the last of it. Open the door and give us the rest. We've found some in almost every house we've visited."

"Yeah, we've seen how you treat the hosts."

"Boy, you best open this door or it's going to get ugly."

Hank opened his mouth to talk again when Trip jumped across the room and tackled him to the ground. He pulled Hank along, crawling toward Gretchen.

"Are they—" Gretchen started to say, but Trip pulled her off the bed and she fell to the floor with a thud. "What the hell?"

Gunfire crashed through the front door and through the walls. The front door splintered and then shattered from a blunt kick. The man with the mustache marched into the front room. Trip rolled over and fired at the man, striking him in the chest. As he stumbled to the side, the man behind him shot at Trip, striking the floor right at their feet.

Hank breathed hard and his pulse pounded in his ears, quieting the commands from the people entering the house. They screamed at them and fired several more shots. Hank steadied his gun and thought about grinners. He struck the first man in the head and then the other one behind him.

They fell to the floor and the mustache man got back to his feet feeling his chest. He tossed an object to the floor and it landed next to Gretchen's bedroom door. Hank lunged away from it and got behind the bed.

The object exploded in a bright light and thunderous sound. The concussion pulsed through Hank and he struggled for his next breath. *This is it. This is when they kill us.*

He pulled himself up to get a line of sight over the bed. Mustache man stood over his dad and fired a shot into him. Hank screamed and fired, striking him in the neck and then several more shots to the head.

He searched for the fourth man, but he fled in their truck.

Hank jumped around the bed and next to his dad. "No, no, Dad! What do I do?"

Blood oozed from his gut and Trip blinked and held his hands. "I can't see." The flash grenade had been much closer to Trip and he'd taken the brunt of it.

Gretchen rolled over and pulled up Trip's shirt. "You are such a fool. Why did you do that?"

"I had to protect you," he said.

Hank felt the blood leave his face, seeing the bullet hole in his gut. "What do I do, Gretchen?" He moved his hands close to the wound and then Trip groaned. Hank pulled his hands back.

"Hospitals are full. I think you know what you need to do, Hank. Take him to Vanar."

Grabbing the radio from Trip's pocket, he called for help. "Trip's been shot!" He stammered over the words and pressed the button again. "I need help, my dad's been shot. We're at Gretchen's!"

"I'm coming right now," Minter answered.

Trip coughed and looked at Hank. "Son, don't worry about me. I'm ready for her, I'm ready to join her."

"Don't talk like that." He glared at the dead guys on Gretchen's family room floor—all this over being greedy and stupid. Trip was right, they should have shot them first. Then his dad wouldn't be laying on the floor, bleeding out. Over the next few minutes, Gretchen and Hank formed a tourniquet with her first aid kit.

Minter ran into the house and slid to a stop next to Trip. He held a gun in one hand and glanced around.

"The last one ran off."

Minter nodded. "Trip, you hear me?" He coughed and nodded his head. "I'm grabbing the quad out of Gretchen's garage. We'll be able to drive you right to the stone with it. I'll be right back."

Hank sat next to his dad and watched his rapid breathing. He heard a quad rev up and Minter drove it next to the front door. He ran into the house and looked to Hank. "Do you know the code for Harris?"

"Yes, I think so."

"Take your dad to the stone right now. It's his only chance."

Determined, Hank grabbed his dad with Minter's help and sat him on the quad. His arms hung over the handle bars. Hank got up and sat behind him.

"Go, Hank, and don't stop for nothing," Minter said, and patted him on the back.

Hank pushed his thumb on the gas and steered the quad onto the dirt road, picking up speed; his dad slumped on the handlebars. "Hang in there, Dad. I'm getting help." He glanced back to make sure no one was following him. Shifting into fifth gear, he passed Joey's house. Not much further.

CHAPTER 10

A CONVOY OF BIG RIGS had been deployed well ahead of Samantha's arrival. Per Zach, they would be all set up and waiting. She took off the headphones and listened to the roar of the engines. The sound was almost relaxing now, a mixture of blades chopping the air and a large motor bellowing its constant grind.

She glanced at her phone, no new messages from Zach. He was somewhere in Europe, setting up distribution channels. She was so proud of him for breaking down the walls of bureaucracy and getting the medicine to the people.

Marge sat across from her, staring at her hands.

"Marge," Samantha said. When she didn't look up, she put on her headset. "Marge."

She gazed up. "Yes, Miss Samantha?"

"Who told you to address me as Miss Samantha?"

Marge's gaze widened and she shook her head. "I—I thought you wanted to be called that."

"So, Zach doesn't have some rule about it?"

"No, Miss Samantha."

"Is there a rule about not telling me about the rules?" Samantha felt like it was a long shot, but they had time to kill.

"No, not at all." Marge looked like she wanted to jump from the helicopter. How she must have loathed being forced into the position of Samantha's assistant.

Not able to decide if she believed Marge, she gave up for the time being. "It's going to be okay. We're about to save a city."

"Have you seen LA on the news? It doesn't look like a safe place."

"Don't worry, me and my men will be there," the man holding a machine gun interrupted.

Samantha recognized him from the trip to Preston. Kind of cute, actually. He caught her looking at him and he studied his boots. "What's your name?" She found it amusing when people were nervous around her. Power was a strange feeling, like a drug pumping into your veins. The more you had, the more you took. The strange thing was, power was given to you by the very people you controlled.

"Derek."

"Well, thanks for not calling me Miss Samantha."

Derek winced at the comment and gripped his gun.

"Five minutes until we land," the pilot announced.

One of the largest cities in the nation spread in every direction. Plumes of smoke lifted from several areas. It was technically her first trip to LA, but they'd all escaped from LA on Ryjack last year. She squinted at the people below, surrounding an area blocked with big rigs parked in a circle.

"Don't tell me we're landing in that."

"Yes, Miss Samantha."

"You all need to stop that, for real. I'd rather you call me turd lady or something."

Marge looked up with a smile and she saw Derek smirking. They were keeping a secret.

The pilot spoke over the airwaves. "One minute, we're setting down."

The helicopter lowered to the middle of the big rig circle on a soccer field. The crowd moved like an ocean against the rigs. There must be tens of thousands—nothing like the crowds in Preston.

She took a deep breath and let it out slowly. "Let's be safe and get in and out quickly."

"Yes, Miss Sam—"

Samantha held up a finger and Marge stopped.

The helicopter landed and Derek ushered her to a staircase leading to the top of a big rig. The metal on top crinkled under her heels and she tiptoed to the podium.

The crowd roared at her presence. They might have seen her on TV from Preston. It had already reached a billion views on YouTube. If power was a drug, she was an addict.

"Hello, LA!" Samantha yelled, opening her arms in greeting. She felt comfortable this time, behind the mic. The crowd roared. She heard them yelling for the cure and as she gazed at all the people below her, she paused to take in their horrifying appearance. Many were coughing, some were even being held up by others. They were dirty, greasy, and her heart went out to them. This was only one of twenty such circle rigs set up around the city. The others were projecting her image onto the sides of the rigs.

"Do you have the cure?" A woman yelled.

Samantha tried to find the owner of the voice but gave up and addressed the crowd as a whole. "Yes, we have the cure and you will be one of the first cities to receive it. You can look at the success at Preston, where there was a hundred percent recovery rate. It is safe and it is free. Courtesy of ZRB."

The crowd cheered and pushed against her rig. The podium jostled and shook in front of her. She gripped the sides of it to steady herself.

"We're dying out here!"

More people yelled out obscenities. She felt the shock of the moment and steadied herself. They weren't giving her power, they wanted to take from her and the shift in the crowd's energy was startling. Her lips moved close to the microphone. "We're losing the world. We're losing everything we have held dear: our jobs, our food, our loved ones. We're losing, aren't we?"

The crowd silenced and stopped moving. They were listening, but she only had them for the second. She would have to earn their trust, her next words were vital. All eyes gazed up at her, waiting.

"We at ZRB are going to stop the losses, starting with you." She pointed down at the crowd and went back on script. "We want to bring the world together, united, to end the Cough. I don't want to lose another friend. I don't want to see children going hungry. I've personally endured loss over the past year, and it almost crushed my spirit. I almost gave into it all..."

She veered off script and looked away from the prompter. "I want you to look to the people around you. They have families, dreams, dads, and moms, they are as human as you are, and I expect you to treat them as such. We have enough cure for everyone, but if you try and ransack us, we all lose again. I'm not sick, but I am sick of losing to this illness. Now, please, people of LA, let's kick this cough in the balls and take a win."

The crowd roared and cheered. Some yelled her name and applauded.

Samantha waved to the crowd and then waited for them to quiet down. "I have a message for the rest of the world. Keep the hope, we're coming to you soon."

The crowd's noise diminished as she stepped down the ladder on the inside of the big rig circle.

"That was pretty good," Marge said, keeping pace with her to the helicopter.

She glanced at Marge for a second. If she believed it, maybe they would as well. The truth was, Samantha didn't know how to get it to the rest of the world in time. She had no real idea of how many vials they had. The big rigs today carried about twenty million. They went double of the city's population to accommodate the floods of people from the other surrounding cities.

She was sure the government would be taking samples from their stock, probably to dissect it and replicate it. Zach thought the whole idea amusing and said no one would be able to duplicate it for years. So, it was on their shoulders to do the job.

She put on her headphones as the helicopter lifted off the grassy field and over the circle of big rigs.

"*Incoming*," was blurted through her headphones.

She saw bright lights shooting out the sides of the helicopter like a hundred flares. The helicopter leaned hard to one side as the motor roared in fury, the maneuver pushing it to its limits. She held onto her seatbelt and heard a whistling sound, then an explosion shook the helicopter.

Alarms blared into her headphone and she felt the copter spinning in a circle. The buildings and sky spun around with increasing speed. Her butt lifted off the seat.

"Brace, brace, brace," the pilot screamed.

Marge's hair raised up around her ears as she screamed.

They impacted on the ground and Marge collapsed into her chair. Pain shot through Samantha's body and smoke flooded the helicopter. She heard the crackling of fire, but her arms and legs wouldn't work the way she wanted them to. Screaming as smoke filled the cabin, she breathed it in. Samantha tried to cough it out. She had to pull herself together; she couldn't die like this.

CHAPTER 11

JOEY STARED AT THE BIG rigs lined up like some old west wagon circle. Men and women in white moved around on the inside of the circle. He also spotted the many armed men around the trucks. He couldn't believe how much Marcus accomplished in one year. He already had an army and a company to hide behind.

"You think this is where she'll land?" Poly asked.

"Everything pointed to this one area," Julie said. While scanning the ZRB servers for information, she'd found the shipment schedule and this location was marked with Samantha's name. At that point, they'd changed direction and went straight to LA in time for the shipment to arrive.

"You're sure Marcus is in Europe?" Joey asked.

"If this Zach guy is Marcus, then yes. I'm sure."

"Who else could he be?"

"Look." Poly pointed to a brigade of helicopters moving over the city.

Joey followed the pack as it approached. One broke off from the pack and landed in the middle of the circle of rigs.

The people around them coughed and pushed forward. A man with a black hat and black clothes moved closer to the podium rising from the top of a big rig. They were at the right place. They pushed forward, but the crowd pushed them back, not letting them get closer. Between the coughs and conversations he doubted he could have gotten Samantha's attention anyway.

A few minutes later, Samantha appeared. She looked good, in designer clothes and all done up. Sharp and professional. It only served to further his anger. What kind of pressure did Marcus have on her to make her do this?

Samantha never looked in their direction, even as they yelled her name. She went through a rousing speech that felt genuine, and he felt the shot she threw at him. The crowd cheered and chanted her name. Then she descended into the big rig. The people with those vial guns, like Poly had, begun to inject people at a rapid pace. It was hard to argue with it, but Marcus was providing a service, he was saving a city and many lives. Too bad they didn't know he was the one who started the virus to begin with.

What quicker way to gain power over a new world than to become its hero? But no one had even seen this Zach guy yet, the only face of ZRB had been Samantha. He needed to get Samantha out.

"You guys ready?" Joey asked.

They nodded their heads. It wouldn't be easy to get past the guards, but every second he waited felt as if he was that much closer to losing Samantha. He pushed through the crowd, not getting anywhere fast.

"No cutting you stupid kids."

Frustrated, Joey stopped and looked across the crowd, trying to find a spot where he could get to Samantha.

"Look." Lucas tugged on Joey's jacket and pointed. "The helicopter's taking off."

He watched the helicopters hover above the big rigs. They were too late, they didn't even get close. He cursed himself for his stupid plan. Did he really think he could get to Samantha so easily?

Scanning the city skyline, he tried to come up with some way to get a message to Samantha. A motion on top of the building next to them grabbed his attention. Maybe ten stories high, he saw a man on the edge with a gun, dressed in all black. Joey searched the area around them and found more men lingering in the background. One had a rifle poking out of the bottom of his jacket.

"They're going to attack," Joey said. "We've got to stop them!"

His friends look confused and before he could explain, a missile streaked toward the helicopter. The pilot made a sharp turn and deployed a massive burst of flares from its side, but the missile struck the back end of the copter and it went into a tailspin.

"Samantha's in there!" Joey screamed and he formed a new path toward the falling helicopter. It crashed inside the big rig circle. He couldn't see anything but a plume of smoke billowing up.

The soldiers in black descended on the crowd, heading for the crash site. The ZRB security guards opened fire on the assault, but the snipers on top of the buildings plucked them off one at a time. The sounds of gunfire stopped. The crowd surged against the big rigs. They didn't run away from the assault, they needed the cure.

Joey held Poly's hand and pulled her toward the action. He unbuttoned his jacket to get access to his guns if needed. The men in black climbed over the trucks and landed on the inside of the circle. Joey lost any courtesies as he plowed sick people to the ground in his pursuit.

A large black helicopter appeared and hovered. Smoke from Samantha's craft swirled around it. A basket dropped and then moments later he saw her . . . Samantha stuffed in the basket, hanging from the helicopter in midair.

The crowd exploded in anger, many taking videos with their cell phones. A person in the crowd fired his gun at the helicopter taking Samantha, until his head exploded. Joey stopped and glanced at the snipers on top of the building. He stopped Poly from advancing and just shook his head. She fumed and pulled at him, but he wasn't going to let them die. Julie and Lucas saw the same thing and stopped next to them. Whatever was going to happen to Samantha, had already happened.

They were too late and he felt his chin trembling as he watched her being dragged behind the copter. They had her. Someone else had done what they'd hoped to do; someone with a lot more resources and manpower.

"They took her." Julie held her hand over her mouth and watched the blank sky, maybe hoping the copter would return and drop their friend in their lap.

A woman in white was flung out of a big rig and a man in black stepped the open door and slammed it shut. This repeated at all the big rigs and Joey stepped back, watching the crowd going into crazy mode. They pounded on the doors and screamed. A few men in black jumped to the top of the rigs and threw objects into the crowd. They exploded in a bright flash and soon, the need for a cure and the need to live to get a cure was crossed. People turned and ran from the rigs.

"We need to get out of here," Joey said.

The big rigs started up and the first one pulled ahead. People dodged the rig and it moved closer to the road.

The rig sat its front tires on the asphalt road when it exploded. The cab engulfed into flames and then the next rig and the one after that, soon all the rigs that formed the circle were flaming balls of fire. Many of the men in black never got out and some burned on the ground just outside of the door.

"What the hell?" Lucas said. "He was just giving it to everyone. Why steal it?"

"Why steal Samantha?" Julie asked. "Something bigger is going on here."

People pushed against them, running for their lives. Joey held Poly's hand and jogged to the center of the street. The crowd thinned and he spotted a McDonalds and pointed at it. The crowd thinned as they approached the establishment. The glass front door lay open and shattered.

Lucas stepped over the glass and into the shell of a restaurant. "Guess they're open."

The store looked as if someone had ransacked the whole thing. Even the napkins and ketchup buckets were ripped out. They cleared a booth and sat. Poly and Joey faced Julie and Lucas. Tears welled up in Julie's eyes and she wiped them with her sleeve.

"We couldn't do a damned thing out there. This sucks," Poly said.

"Julie, see if you can find her," Joey said.

She sucked up the snot in her nose and pulled out her Panavice, scrolling the pages. Her mouth opened and she stared at the screen. Turning it so the group could see. "Recognize it?"

"Same one that took Samantha," Poly answered.

"Yep, but this is a stealth helicopter, built by one country in the world. The US."

"Wait, you're saying our government captured Samantha?" Lucas asked.

"It wasn't just that, they were trying to take the cure as well," Julie said.

Joey leaned back on the booth seat trying to absorb the information. Why would the government want Samantha? She was just the face of the distributor. Plus shooting down the copter could have killed her. "Can you see where they took her?"

"Yes." Julie scrolled her screen for a few minutes. "They took her to the Miramar Air Force base in San Diego." Her face sagged as she stared at the screen.

"What is it?" Lucas asked.

"There's no record of an authorized kidnapping. Nothing talking about seizing the cure. I think these soldiers went rogue, or are some kind of black ops."

Lucas put his hands behind his head and laughed. "This is crazy."

"After all we've been through, is there any limit to crazy?" Julie blurted out.

He lowered his hands to his lap and sunk in his seat. "Well, it might be easier to get her back from them than Marcus."

"As stupid as that sounds, you may be right," Julie said. "I can get into any military network, but that's something I can't do with ZRB." She shook her head as she stared at the screen. "I don't see any record of anything at Miramar involving this. I don't like it at all."

"Are they transporting her out of there?"

"I don't know, but they may be hiding her if they do."

Joey spoke up, leaning forward in the seat. "How long to get there by car?"

"Probably two hours or so. Depending on the roads," Julie said. "Wait, I found something. There's been internal chatter about a group of soldiers led by a man they call Judge. This group is off the grid. They're acting on their own."

"What do they want from her?" Joey asked.

Julie stared at him. "She's the VP of ZRB, I am sure they want what the whole world wants . . . the cure."

CHAPTER 12

THE WIND BLEW AGAINST SAMANTHA'S face and panic set in as she realized they weren't going to bring her all the way into the helicopter. She thought at first they were there to rescue her, but now she knew they were taking her. Zach would never allow this to happen. They left her strapped to the steel gurney, but she cocked her head to get a view of the city below. Just then, the first rig blew up. She felt the heat from it and then the helicopter moved.

Terror overwhelmed Samantha and she continued to scream as the gurney swayed next to the door. She was sure at any second she would disconnect, or the straps holding her in place would give way. The massive wind blew the tears from her eyes and streaked them back to her ears. Her throat felt hoarse as she screamed at the men behind her. She closed her eyes and tried to gather some dignity if this was going to be the end.

She thought of her mom. When Samantha had a bad day, her mom saw it in her face. She'd sit her down on the couch and put on a silly daytime soap opera. Her mom would sit behind her and comb her hair, trying to catch Samantha up on what was happening. It always made her feel better, even if she couldn't care less that Joan was sleeping around on Terrence.

She hummed the tune to her mom's favorite soap and kept her eyes closed. The noise of wind and the roaring of the helicopter motor drowned out the sound, but she felt the vibrations and used her mind to fill in the rest. She began to have rational thoughts and loosened one hand.

She opened her eyes and gazed up at the black helicopter with sharp angles all around it. It didn't have any markings and it looked futuristic, like those stealth bombers the government used.

She blinked and the wind dried her eyes out almost instantly. She slammed them shut and ignored the gritty feeling. She thought of Ashley and how she'd said the president contacted her directly. It couldn't be a coincidence. Ashley must have told them what they were planning on doing.

The helicopter skimmed the beach line and another big city came into view. It seemed like forever before they finally slowed down and hovered over a large airport. Samantha took deep breaths and felt happy to be still.

The helicopter landed on the tarmac and a dozen men ran up with machine guns pointed at her. The soldiers rushed to pull her to the ground and undo each strap holding her in place.

"Hey, easy." They squeezed her arms and yanked her from the restraints. "Why are you doing this?" she screamed.

Six men held her and tied her hands and legs together with zip ties. Her body never touched the ground and the men never said a word.

"What the hell is going on?" Samantha demanded.

"He'll tell you soon enough."

"Who's going to tell me what?"

The men carried her like a log toward a large hangar. She stopped struggling to save herself the pain from the ties cutting into her skin. When they entered the side door of the immense building, a voice sounded from her right.

"Put her down."

They sat her down on a steel chair but left her constraints on. She felt the thin zip tie digging into her wrists. Frantically looking around, she took in all the uniformed men surrounding her and never felt so alone. She wished Zach would come crashing into the hangar with his machine guns. Too bad he was in Europe somewhere, trying to save them all.

A man in a suit walked toward her, an older man with gray hair and black, shiny shoes. He eyed the men around her and nodded his head. They moved away as he approached.

She sat upright in her seat and tried to look the part of a VP.

"Samantha Roslin?" The contempt in his voice made her name sound like a dirty word.

"Yes, and who do you think you people are, stuffing me in a helicopter and flying me across the state like some animal? I'm an American citizen and I have rights."

"I'm sorry if you were harmed in any way. I'm Judge Spencer, but most of the guys here call me Judge. We brought you here because we want something from you. You give it to us and we leave. Give us trouble and well, things won't be so fun for you. "

"You're threatening me? Do you know who I am?" Samantha tried to quell her anger.

Judge grabbed a steel chair from next to a table and scraped it across the floor to sit in front of her. "You've had an interesting life, Samantha Roslin. Being born on the same day as five other kids—they even called you the Preston Six. Not very inventive, but cute."

"We didn't name ourselves, some reporter did."

"Ah yes, well sometimes the reporters like to put a name on things, don't they?"

Samantha huffed and raised her bounded hands. "Is this necessary?"

Judge nodded his head to the soldier standing behind her.

Once her hands were cut free, she rubbed her wrists and stared at the red marks. She wondered how Zach would react to those marks.

"Last year, you and the Preston Six went missing for several weeks and then you all showed back up at the same time. Where did you go?"

Samantha glanced up at Judge and wondered if this was part of her trial or just some small talk to get the words flowing. If she'd told him the truth, they never would believe it. "We sort of ran away. We traveled to a few places but then ran out of money and the will to continue."

"And in this time, did you or any of the Six have contact with Zach Ryan Baker?"

"No."

"Can you tell me how you became employed with ZRB?"

"They were at a job fair at my school and recruited me."

"Interesting, do you know that your school was the only job fair they have ever attended?"

"No, I didn't." She struggled with what that meant. Maybe it was some trial job fair for them, like an experiment. Samantha used her free hands to stroke some of the knots out of her ratted up hair. "Do you have any idea how terrifying it is to dangle from the bottom of that helicopter?"

"You don't get to ask me questions." Judge's hand balled up in a fist on his knee. His face turned a light shade of red and he looked to be holding back a full-blown fit. Samantha waited for him to ask the next question. "Why did they hire you, and at which position?"

"I'm not answering these questions until you tell me exactly what the hell you want." She felt good about the comment.

Judge leaned back in his chair with a smile. "Do you know any rich people?"

"What?"

"Rich people. You know, the Bill Gates and Warren Buffets of the world."

"No," Samantha said, confused as to where he was going with it.

"But you've heard of them?"

"Yes."

"Well, the people I work for are the ones who decide those people are allowed to be rich. You won't find their names on any Forbes list because they own the magazine. They own whatever it is that they want and every person of great wealth gets to know this universal truth at some point. Zach has avoided them by some very cunning maneuvers and has upset my bosses to no end. They cannot allow for Zach to continue what he is doing, unchecked. Now please, let me finish up my questioning here."

Samantha nodded. These people didn't want the money, they wanted the power behind the cure or a cut of it. This was extortion and Samantha tightened up in her chair, glancing at the armed men around the room. She couldn't get out of this room if she had Zach and the rest of the six with her.

Judge crossed his leg and placed his hands over his knee, holding it in place. "You're the VP and heading up the distribution of the cure. But Samantha, you're nineteen, you have no experience running a company. Why would Zach choose you?"

Samantha shifted in her metal chair and tried to hide her inner struggle. She valued herself and what she was capable of. She had worth and she didn't like for one second this man insinuating she didn't. Images of her hunkering behind the rest of the Six flashed in her mind. She was her own woman now, she didn't need them. "I was the best person for the job."

"I think you are an amazing, beautiful, young woman, but there has to be more to this story. Were you and Zach in a relationship?"

"No. I got promotions on my merits."

"We have a source saying you were seen kissing."

"Who, Ashley? Wait, are you the ones who sent that group of soldiers yesterday?"

"Don't ask me another question. Don't do it." The veins in his neck bulged and his fist shook. After a moment, he loosened his fingers and plastered a weak smile on his face.

Samantha realized she was in a life or death conversation with a mad man and slumped in her seat. "I'm sorry. No more questions."

"Good. Now please, help me understand what it is you do at ZRB."

Samantha went over her role as an organizer of the distribution of the cure and how she was to be the face of ZRB. Judge Spencer nodded and took interest in her answers. She made sure not to ask any questions in return and watched Judge's body language as she felt at any second she was going to have to protect herself from his attacks.

"Now that we have an understanding of what it is you do, why don't you tell me more about your boss, Zach?"

"I have a feeling you know more than I do about him," Samantha said.

"Yes, we have all the records showing his life. Dated purchases, parents' birth and death certificates, high school diploma . . . all found, all legit." Samantha's mouth opened to ask a question, only to close it as Judge raised an eyebrow. "But there's a problem. How can a man who appears to have come from meager beginnings, accomplish what he has in the span of one year?"

Samantha frowned at the information. What was he trying to say? That Zach was some ghost who popped into existence? She pursed her lips together, and made sure to appear doubtful. Let them think their weak tactics of getting her to turn on Zach worked. She knew him better than any person in the world.

A smug look came across Judge's face. "Something isn't right about this guy. A very dangerous game he's playing and you're just another pawn in his plan. Can you see that now?

This man is not the one who should have sole control of the cure. I need your help to get to him, to make him understand the stakes at which he is playing."

"He's trying to save the world, not control it."

Judge laughed and looked around at his men who also laughed. "Do you really believe that?"

She couldn't look Judge in the face and instead focused on a button on his lapel. Two triangles with a circle between them. "Yes, he's making a better world."

Judge wiped a hand over his face and kept smiling. "So, we have a simple task for you. Make contact with your boss and in exchange for your life, we want him to sign over fifty-one percent of his company to my people. A very generous offer that will skyrocket Zach to the top of the Forbes list, a mile ahead of number two."

Judge waved to the person behind her. "We have your cell phone here and see you have communicated with him recently, sweet little texts you guys sent each other."

Samantha sneered at Judge and grabbed her phone from the guy holding it to her.She sucked in a breath and stared at the screen. What could she possibly say? *Hey, honey, these guys are threatening me if you don't hand over controlling equity in ZRB*. And what if he chose the company? She had a sick feeling of being stuck as an option to another man. Her hands sweat and shook as her thumb hovered over the screen. "I can't do this."

Judge's eye twitched and he shot out of his chair, face turning red. He raised a clenched fist over her face and she crunched up in fear.

"We can't hit her," the soldier from behind Judge said. He stepped toward them. It was the winker. "It's not right." The soldier regarded her with a soft face and expressive eyes. "It's okay, Miss Samantha, you can contact him." He gave her a quick wink and then Judge shoved him to the ground.

"Don't ever interrupt me." He kicked the soldier in the stomach and then again in the face.

None of the other soldiers looked their way. They kept to their routes, pacing and watching the building.

Samantha shook her hands and wanted to be far away from Judge. He turned to face her and swiped his hand over his sweaty forehead. He stomped back to his seat and slammed it closer to her, so when he sat down his face was a foot away from hers. She felt the heat from his body and the stench of his breath on her face. She recoiled, but he tapped the screen with his finger.

"Put in the message, we've already sent him all the paperwork."

Samantha stared at the digital keys, anything was better than the man's face. Then it struck her. The soldier had called her *Miss* Samantha. She shot a quick glance at the man on the floor.

Putting her fingers to the keys, she typed in the note telling Zach of the situation.

Judge smiled and read each words as she typed it. "See? That wasn't too hard."

Samantha slumped in her chair. She'd wanted to put up a fight, but the Miss Samantha comment threw her. The man must have been sending her a message from Zach. She fidgeted her fingers and felt like a traitor.

What if the man on the floor had just been part of their plan? They could have known about her name thing and he used it to give her an edge of comfort? She felt as if she might throw up. If she had just handed over Zach into a trap, she didn't know how she could live with herself.

She stared at the screen, waiting for his response. It dinged and his message displayed.

Zach: Hand the phone to Judge.

She stared at the words and then handed the phone over. She had to trust in Zach. He would know how to get her out of this mess better than anyone.

Judge's face was smiling as he typed into the screen. A few more dings as Zach's texts came across the screen, and his face changed, taking the blood out of it at first and then contorting it with rage. He got out of his seat and slammed the phone onto the floor. It shattered on the ground and then he stomped on it repeatedly. In one motion, he reached over and smacked the side of her head. She blocked most of it with her hand, but it sent chills and thumps of pain down her spine. Her eyes hurt from the impact and she blinked to get her vision clear again. She rubbed the side of her head and slammed her eyes shut.

What did Zach text him?

"Guess your life isn't as valuable to him as we thought."

"What did he say?" Samantha jolted from her seat.

Judge swung and hit her on the side of the head.

Crashing to the floor, Samantha groaned. She grabbed the side of her head and rocked back and forth on the cool concrete. "He's going to kill you for doing this," she said. "He'll find you. You know he will, he's everywhere."

Judge laughed and walked away.

The soldier he'd kicked earlier moved to her side. Samantha expected comfort or help from the man, but he grabbed her and shoved her on her face. She felt zip ties move over her wrists once again. She raised her chin off the floor and stared at the hangar door, waiting. Someone had to come to her rescue, she couldn't die like this. Zach was in Europe and every friend she'd ever had was in Preston. They didn't even know where she was. The fear of dying and no one even knowing it happened, filled her thoughts.

"Miss Samantha," the soldier whispered, "it's time for you to go with me."

CHAPTER 13

"WE NEED TO GO FASTER," Joey said. He was going to lose it if they couldn't get out of this damned traffic. He knew Samantha was in danger and every second they wasted felt like she was one second closer to death.

"Dude, you're seeing the same thing I am." Lucas squeezed the steering wheel with frustration.

Joey sighed. They were the only car heading south. Both sides of the five lane freeway had turned into northbound traffic. Everyone had headed to LA in search for the cure.

"I bet they just want to question her or something," Poly spoke up from the back.

"If they really wanted to question her, they wouldn't have carted her off like that," Joey said a bit testier than intended.

He'd been the one who pushed Samantha away. It was him and his actions alone which were to blame for everything. He just wanted to get her back and make sure she was safe.

Lucas drove on the shoulder and the car bounced over the divots in the dirt. A family walking alongside the highway moved out of the way. The wife held onto her man as he coughed. Their two kids carried large bags on their backs. The wife stared at Joey as they passed. He wanted to get out and hand the last few cures they had to them. He hated having them. It felt as if each person they passed was condemned to death.

As they got further away from LA, the traffic thinned. Less people were driving north on the southbound lane.

Julie gave directions to Lucas as he veered onto another freeway. She called out the exit and they were finally on Miramar Road. Joey spotted the large air force base that held Samantha.

THE DOOR FLUNG OPEN AND the twilight bled into the small metal shed. A man grabbed Samantha and pulled her to her feet. Adjusting to the light, she surveyed the group of soldiers surrounding her with guns drawn.

"Bunch of tough men, aren't ya?" she spouted with her hands tied behind her back. "What are you going to do, shoot me? Do I look dangerous? Do I look like a person who needs to be shot?"

A few of the men lowered their guns.

One of the men leaned close to her and cut the zip tie. The movement made her think they might be letting her go, until he took her hands behind her back, pushing one high. She grimaced as the pain shot through her shoulder. She wanted to spit on the man next to her. She wanted to stomp on him and make him pay for treating her like some dog.

He pulled on her other arm and she felt metal cuffs locking her hands behind her back.

"Am I that terrifying?"

None of them answered and some of them looked away.

She stared down the one brave enough to look her in the eyes.

The soldier behind her shoved a cloth bag over her head. A smidgen of light came through and she saw the silhouettes of the men surrounding her.

She took a deep breath and fought the urge to run. She knew she couldn't get ten feet with them around her and the bag over her head. "You can't do this!" They didn't answer. She wasn't a human to them, just some animal they were taking out to pasture.

This can't be happening.

But it was. She felt a hand on the back of her neck and she flinched.

"Just stay calm."

She stood still. She knew the voice, the Miss Samantha soldier who took a beating.

"Back away, soldier," another stern voice said.

The silhouette of a man moved toward her. She stepped back and felt the asphalt grinding under her shuffling feet. The man grabbed her at the elbow, yanking until she moved.

Her breath pushed against the black fabric and she wanted to scream. "Get your hands off me!" She pulled her arm free and ran. She couldn't see much, just enough to spot the hole in their line, and ran through it. She ran hard and heard their boots on the tarmac, running after her.

Her shoe caught on something and she plunged to the ground. She tried to land on her side, but with her arms behind her back, she landed on her face.

Crying out, Samantha felt warm blood on her arm and face. She moaned over the pain and tried to lift her face off the asphalt. The black cloth-covered-world swam in front of her and she felt many hands touching her body.

She sobbed and screamed at the men as blood flowed into her eye and she desperately wanted her hands back. She wanted to wipe the blood away. Her face felt hot and throbbed with pain. The cloth over her head was now wet with her blood, making it even harder to get fresh air.

They yanked her off the ground. She felt hands on her legs and arms as they carried her like a pig on a stick. More blood dripped on the cloth hood and smeared over her face. The smell of it filled her nose.

"You can't do this." She wanted to scream, but it came out gargled.

"I think she's hurt," the Miss Samantha soldier said.

"I don't give a rat's ass if she's hurt. Judge gave us orders."

"We shouldn't be doing this. We're not killers."

"What do you call what happened in Scottsdale?"

"It's not the same, she's not hurting anyone. She's just a kid."

"If you don't want to end up like Parker, you'll keep your mouth shut and do your job."

"But—"

"Not another word."

They didn't say anything else.

She saw glimmers of motion below her. Feet moving, pavement gliding by. They fell into a marched rhythm and her body bounced along. The cuffs dug into her wrists and they were hurting her shoulder, but her fear was overwhelming the pain.

"Please," she whispered.

Nothing.

"I'm just a front person. I'm nothing in the company."

They kept marching.

Someone's voice warbled over a radio, "We've got a group entering from the north gate."

Hope.

They stopped and dropped her on the ground.

"He's coming for me. You're all going to die," she said and spit some of the blood from her mouth.

"Jennings, Cooper, take her behind the hangar. You three take positions along the side. Mooks, can you get high?"

"Aye."

"Go."

She felt two sets of hands grab and haul her. She kicked her feet, trying to keep up but mostly they dragged her. They plopped her against a steel building.

"Can you take this damned bag off my head?"

The bag was gone. The soldier, wide-eyed, stared at her.

Is it that bad?

The other soldier looked. "Oh damn, Miss Samantha," he struggled with the words and closed his eyes in fury. He shook his head and positioned himself next to the building, gun pointed toward the tarmac.

"We should use her for bait."

"She could get killed."

"We're going to kill her anyways, man. What's with you?"

Her only hope glanced at her and shook his head. He yanked a dagger out from his side and stabbed the other soldier in the throat.

The soldier gurgled and fired his gun, striking the Miss Samantha soldier in the chest. Blood splattered her face and the two men fell together. Neither moved.

Samantha staggered to her feet, wanting to scream. She wanted to cover her mouth and wipe the blood from her face. The one man who gave her a glimmer of hope lay dead before her. She cringed and pulled at her cuffs.

"Pete, report. Gunshots heard," his radio blurted out.

"We've got a bird incoming," another person on the radio said.

Samantha turned and saw a black plane landing on the tarmac. She knew that plane. It had a ZRB logo on the side. He'd come for her. She wanted to run to the plane and jump into his arms.

"Mooks, take it out. Free fire, men. Nothing gets on or off that plane."

A rocket launched from a nearby tower, heading straight for the black plane landing on the runway.

"No," Samantha cried out. A flash came from the plane and the rocket exploded at a safe distance. She breathed a deep sigh of relief.

Automatic gunfire sounded. She ducked down next to the steel building. The bullets sparked off the plane. The plane turned toward the oncoming fire. More flashes burst from the front of the plane and a loud hum sounded. The bullets crashed through the steel buildings and Samantha ducked low, trying to protect herself from falling debris. The plane turned toward her and continued to fire into the buildings.

In thirty seconds, silence.

She slid her back on the steel wall to prop herself up on her feet. Using her one eye not filled with blood, she watched the airplane door open and a ladder fold out. She spotted Zach standing at the door. Taking a step toward him, she heard someone call out from behind.

"Samantha?"

She didn't need to look to know who was there, even if it seemed impossible. "Joey," she whispered, turning to see him. Her heart ached. He looked so good in the twilight.

His face contorted with fear and anger. "My God, what happened?" He rushed to her.

She looked back to Zach, standing on the stairs of the plane. Turning to Joey, she said, "You shouldn't be here."

He touched her hair, pulling it from her face. She would have smacked his hand away if they weren't stuck behind her back. He didn't have the right to touch her.

"Samantha. . . ." his voice cracked. "I'm so sorry. Let's get you out of here."

"I have a ride already."

He glanced at the plane. "We were about to take out those men. The men who did this to you."

"But you were too late, weren't you?"

Joey pulled his shirt off. "You're bleeding."

She looked away from his body. He blotted the cut above her eye. She winced but let it happen. It had been bothering her since she fell. "I have to go."

"Back to *him*?" Joey glared at Zach standing at the top of the staircase. It was too far for Zach to see the glare.

"Where else would I go?"

"With us." Joey looked behind him.

There they were. Lucas, Julie, and Poly. Lucas nodded and Poly smiled. Samantha felt the years' long connection with them, but it also brought on the pain.

"No, the world needs me, and more importantly, someone else needs me." She glanced at Zach. *Why is he standing there and not running to me?*

"We are not the Preston Six without you, Samantha," Joey said.

"Is that what you're not? Listen, Joey," she felt the tears building in her eyes and it stung badly with the mixture of blood, "this isn't just about us. The world is dying and I am going to do everything I can to save it. After these men tried to take everything Zach and I have created together, I'm even more determined." She turned and started walking toward the plane.

"Wait," Julie called out. She rushed up and hugged Samantha. "You look terrible," she whispered.

Samantha didn't know if it was tears or blood streaking down her face, but she didn't care. She wanted to enjoy this moment with her best friend. Even if she sided with them, she missed her terribly.

Julie didn't let go. "He's not who you think he is," she continued to whisper. "That's Marcus Malliden standing on that plane."

Samantha tried to push away with her shoulder, but Julie held her tight. She turned to face her. "You lying bitch. That man is saving the world."

Julie let go, looking as if she'd been burned. "I'm sorry, he's using you. It's some kind of sick game. All of this is. Who do you think *created* the Cough? This is the same virus that took over Vanar all those years ago. In a few seconds, we are going to kill him."

"No, you're wrong! Come with me and meet him. He is not Marcus." Samantha turned and jogged to the plane trying to keep her balance with her hands still cuffed behind her back.

Zach ran down the stairs and met her halfway. He frowned and grasped her face. She saw the tears welling in his eyes. Julie stayed back a few steps, staring at Zach with her mouth open, a dumbfounded look on her face.

"I'll make every person responsible for this pay for what they did to you." He turned his attention to Julie. "Hello, Julie. It's a pleasure to finally meet another one of the Six. Oh, and I see the rest over there."

"You're not Marcus," Julie delivered the words slowly.

Zach looked perplexed. "I'm sorry, I guess I didn't introduce myself. I'm Zach Ryan Baker." He extended his hand. Julie kept her hands to her side.

Joey, Poly, and Lucas ran up next to her. Each took in Zach, seeing him for who he was. Joey lowered his hand from his gun and shared the same shocked look as Poly and Lucas.

"So good to finally meet you all," Zach said. "I hope you don't mind if I get Samantha treatment for her eye. I fear she may have a concussion as well. Plus, we can get those cuffs off."

Samantha gazed at her friends, they didn't say anything in protest. She badly wanted the cuffs off and she wanted a mirror. She gazed back at Joey who studied Zach and his movements. Did they really think Zach was Marcus? Like she wouldn't know if she was working for the worst person who ever lived? The person who had her dad killed? The idea seemed insane.

"Samantha, please, go inside and get some medical help," Zach pleaded.

She took one last look at her old friends and trotted up the stairs. The nurse rushed her into the plane, while a man stood behind her and removed the cuffs. Her wrists felt raw and she rubbed them fiercely. She hoped her friends were being cordial with Zach. It'd be just like Lucas to say something stupid.

CHAPTER 14

THE MAN APPROACHING THEM WORE a big smile and a face that wasn't Marcus Malliden's. Joey controlled his breath. His hands shook and he fought every urge to rush for Samantha climbing the stairs into the plane.

"I wanted to thank you guys. I know if I hadn't shown up, you'd have taken care of her," Zach said. He even sounded different.

Joey recoiled from the man's hand and reached for his gun.

"You don't want to do that."

Joey stopped. "We know who you are."

Zach's smile changed to a scowl. "I have no idea what you're talking about."

Joey stepped closer to the man. "You might have her fooled, but not us."

"That's right, you think I am this Marcus guy..."

"You must have gotten plastic surgery or something. We have proof." Joey looked to Julie for backup.

Zach waved a dismissive hand in front of Julie. "I don't want to hear it. I'm not who you think I am. All I want to do is protect Samantha." He moved closer to Joey. "You may not believe I'm Zach Baker, but that isn't my problem. Soon, the whole world will be shouting my name from the rooftops. *Thank you, Zach Ryan Baker! Thank you for saving us!*"

"You're crazy. We know you started this disease."

Zach chest-butted Joey and put his face close to his. "If you listen real carefully, there will be one more person screaming my name tonight. *Oh, Zach!*"

Joey swung at the douchebag's face.

Zach grabbed his hand and pushed him to the ground. "See ya, Preston *Four* is it now?" He let go of his hold on Joey and walked toward the plane.

Joey pulled out his gun and fired at the back of his head. Zach didn't flinch and the bullet bounced off his shield.

"See? You have a shield. *Samantha!* He has a shield!"

Zach ran into the plane and the door closed behind him. The motors revved up and the plane's gun moved, pointing at them.

"Run," Joey yelled.

He made sure Poly ran in front of him in case they decided to start shooting. He ran with his shoulder pulled up and his head down as if that would give him any protection. They kept running all the way to the steel hangar. The plane never fired a shot. By the time they looked back out of the hangar, the plane streaked across the sky.

Joey stared at the jet trail it left behind. It was worse than he could have ever imagined. With the knowledge she was given, she still chose to go with him. Zach must have manipulated her, fooled her, fed her lies. He shook his head, trying to put logic where there was none.

"She thinks she's saving the world," Julie said.

"She's searching for love," Poly said.

"Yeah, well he's ending the world. They say love is blind. Is it also stupid?" Julie asked.

Joey held Poly with one arm and kept looking at the sky. He wouldn't accept the loss of Samantha. She was in the arms of the Devil and he planned on getting her back. Marcus, Zach, whatever the guy wanted to call himself, had a plan and Joey was going to do everything he could to stop that plan from happening. If he couldn't get to Samantha, he'd get to his company; he'd find the errors and give Samantha the trails to follow on her own. She had to see it.

"What's our next move?" Lucas asked.

"We need help, we need to get to Harris," Julie said.

"And Travis," Poly added. "I think with our new knowledge, he'll help us."

Joey could only hope.

CHAPTER 15

SAMANTHA FELT THE SUPPLE LEATHER seat and stared at Zach sitting across from her. He didn't retract from her mutilated face. She hadn't had the guts to look in the mirror yet, but she felt the puffiness around the wounds and the bandage over her right eye. Zach's on-plane nurse helped clean up the worst of it. She'd spread white goo all over and then placed a bandage over the side of her face.

"Are you in any pain?"

"No, and thanks for coming to get me," her voice cracked.

"Anything for you."

Samantha lowered her head and then looked out the window. The dark, featureless sky sped by. She stared at the void, thinking of Julie and Joey. Julie had grabbed her and told her Zach was Marcus.

She glanced at Zach.

Marcus was an evil man who'd killed her dad. The man sitting across from her was the sweetest, most caring person she'd ever known. And he had the balls to kill any man to protect her. Marcus wouldn't do such things. Marcus wouldn't find interest in a nineteen-year-old.

Zach watched her with a smile. "What are you thinking?"

She gave him the clean side of her face to look at as she gazed out the window. "Life's complicated, isn't it?"

"You have no idea." He scooted forward in his seat and took her hand in his.

"Zach," she turned to him, exposing her face, "are you who you say you are?"

He frowned and rubbed the top of her hand with his thumb. "Do I seem as if I could be someone else?"

"My friends think you are . . . someone awful."

"Yes, your friends. Interesting bunch. I know one thing though, they love you and they are friends of mine by proxy."

Samantha turned and stared at the window. The world below was collapsing. She had to help those who were suffering. They had to get the cure out to the world by any means necessary. It wasn't about her and Zach saving the world anymore. She just wanted to get back to normal. "I want to start mass distribution of the cure."

"Doesn't take you long to talk shop, does it?"

"I'm serious."

He let go of her hand and leaned back in the seat. "I agree. I was just about to tell you that we are launching our first cure centers in France." He smiled.

"France?"

"I thought that's what you wanted? We're rolling it out to most of Europe over the next week, parts of Asia and South America too."

"What about the United States?"

"The government hasn't been responsive."

"We can't wait for them, Zach. We need to do it ourselves."

"You saw what happened in LA, I nearly lost you." Zach glanced out the window and crossed his leg. "If I try, they will stop me and mess everything up. We want to work with them, but they have to be the ones to meet us halfway. You see that, right?"

"It wasn't the government who took me, but you know that already," Samantha said. "It sounds like you've pissed off the wrong people."

He laughed. "Yes, the world is a fascinating place with so many layers. Most of those layers the average person never gets to see. Did you know there are six people who control most of the world?" He laughed again. "Kind of like the Preston Six."

"They aren't messing around. I think it's going to get worse. I don't think they are going to stop until they control ZRB."

"You let me handle them."

She nodded. She might have told Zach not to bother, but she wanted him to find those men. They needed to pay for what they did to her. "One of them helped me. He kept calling me Miss Samantha."

"I only wished he could have helped more. He was a friend of mine." He gently pushed back a strand of hair and tucked it behind her ear.

"Well, he saved my life."

"I'll make sure his family is well taken care of."

Samantha gazed out the window. "Where are we going?"

"I've grown very fond of you."

She opened her mouth and closed it, smiling sheepishly. "That doesn't answer my question."

"I have a special place I want to show you. I think you'll like it."

SAMANTHA CLASPED THE EDGE OF the marble countertop and leaned closer to the mirror. She inspected her face in the morning light. It couldn't be possible, but there it was, staring back at her. The once large gash, shrunken to a thin red line. The garish bruising turned to just a hint of red over her cheek and eye. She touched it with her hand and felt a hint of pain, but nothing like the throbbing of the night before.

She looked through the bathroom door to see Zach stirring from his sleep. She pulled his bathrobe tighter around herself. Samantha had thought being with Zach would take her mind off of her friends, or the faces of Derek and Marge in the fire fight around the helicopter, but their faces still plagued her mind—maybe even more. She looked back at the mirror, thinking of what brought her there.

The place Zach had wanted to show her was his new cliffside house. She wondered why he built a house so far away from anything. It almost felt familiar to her, but she couldn't place it. Almost like Déjà vu.

Thoughts of Joey and what might have been crept into her consciousness. Sighing, she pushed him from her thoughts. That was another life. Samantha had a man who wanted her, a man who didn't hide from his feelings and was able to express his desires.

She watched in the mirror as Zach made his way across the bedroom floor. Both of his hands caressed her arms and he kissed the back of her neck. A chill shot down her back and she turned for more. Kissing him deep, she felt his hard chest pressing against her.

"I have to go for a while," he said between kisses.

"No," she whimpered.

"You got me thinking last night. I can do more to get the US on board. I have to at least try. Can you stay here and wait for me?"

"I think I better get back to corporate," Samantha said.

"Look at your face." He brushed her cheek with the back of his hand.

Turning around to look in the mirror, she had to search for the damage. "What did that nurse put on me?"

"I don't know, but she's getting a raise." He smiled and wrapped his arms around her waist. "If you want to go back to the office, let me know and I can drop you off there first."

"Where are you going?"

He let go of her and walked over to turn his shower on. It had three heads and looked like something out of the future. "I set up a big meeting."

She turned to face him. "With who?"

"The President of the United States has granted me an audience."

"That's wonderful news." She beamed.

"Well, it doesn't mean we have an agreement, but it's a step in the right direction."

"You better play nice with the POTUS."

"He might be trying to kill me." Zach laughed.

She crunched her face in a question. She was beginning to know his quirks and that sounded like his I'm-joking-but-I'm-really-serious laugh. "If he hurts you, you tell him he'll have me to deal with."

"Hell hath no fury..."

ENTERING THE FRONT DOORS OF ZRB, security waved Samantha past the scanners. The elevator opened on her floor and the office went silent upon her arrival. She stopped and looked around. Faces stared at her as if they were seeing a ghost. She met those stares and they darted back to their screens. Soon, the sound of the office clatter restarted. She walked past the nonsense and opened the door to her office.

The glass door closed behind her and she plopped down on her chair. It wheeled back a few inches.

"Hello, Miss Samantha."

Startled, she jumped out of her chair. "Derek!" She rushed to him and gave him an awkward hug, careful of his injuries. "I didn't even see you there."

"I saw you." His arm hung inside a sling and a bandage covered part of his forehead.

"I thought they killed you."

"They shot me and I fell, hitting my head." His eye's got watery. "I'm sorry they took you. I won't let that happen again."

"What about Marge?" He shook his head and looked at the carpet. "You shouldn't be here. You should be home or something. How can you even think of working in your condition?"

"I begged Zach to keep me on duty. I made a promise to him not to leave your side."

Samantha appreciated his commitment. "Thank you."

He nodded his head and backed up to the corner of the room. "Forget I'm even here."

"I think I'm safe in my own office." Samantha walked over to her desk and opened her purse to pull out an emery board. Her nails looked a mess.

"You need me more than I think you know," Derek said.

"I was just freaking kidnapped, I think I know the importance of protection. And how did it go the last time you were helping?"

Derek looked at the floor. "I won't let that happen again."

She felt bad for her choice of words. "Some things are just out of our control."

"You are right." He moved closer to her. "And you should have some way to defend yourself if needed. Let me show you something." He plucked the file from her hand and pulled out a knife from his side. He proceeded to cut the emery board until it had a sharp end and handed it back to her. "Now you have a weapon."

"Thanks." Samantha took her new weapon and thought it could still function nicely.

"I won't leave unless you tell me to."

She pondered the statement. It was better having his face around than her coworkers. "I don't mind. Though, I may bug you now and then."

"You can't bug me, Miss Samantha."

She sighed at the name and thought about ordering him to call her Samantha or Sam, but she stopped herself and conceded. Had Zach really ordered everyone to call her that? He must have, but why? Some sort of respect thing?

Meandering back to her chair, she sat and opened her laptop. Typing in her password, Prestonsix19, ZRB's primary access page flipped up on the screen. She typed Marge in the personnel search bar. She didn't know her last name, but at least she could send her parents or husband a personal letter or something.

The search came up blank. Not a single Marge worked for ZRB?

She leaned closer and typed in Ashley. Nothing. She sighed and typed in Derek. His face popped up on screen and she read his history. Military turned into a private security specialist. She glanced at him, but he didn't have a look of conversation about him. He looked as if he was trying to look in every direction at the same time. "We're alone, you know?"

"Excuse me if I appear jumpy, but I will consider you in grave danger at all times now."

"Am I, in grave danger?"

"Yes."

Samantha breathed in deep. It wasn't for fear of the comment, but for what it meant. He wasn't going to let off. He was going to be an ever presence of nervous energy. She thought of Zach's relaxed state and longed for it.

The company inbox on her screen displayed a large number on top of the blue square. Odd, that had never been there before. She slid her finger over the screen and tapped the box. It swirled and an email popped up. She leaned forward, staring at the title.

Five plus one makes six.

She tapped the email and a few lines appeared.

I know you don't believe me, but I'll find the evidence. I hope you're ready.
We miss you.
JM

The words felt bold on the screen, as if they had weight. It shouldn't surprise her that Julie was able to get into the ZRB system. She tapped the reply button and the window changed to a reply box. Thinking twice, she closed all the windows and shut the laptop. She wondered what they were up to. If they really thought Zach was Marcus, they'd be plotting against him. They would be doing everything they could to stop him.

Didn't they realize they weren't playing on other planets anymore? They were on Earth, and could undo everything her and Zach had been building. Julie had the technology beyond anything of this world and the rest had the skills to pull off stunts that could really do damage to the company.

She hated thinking of her old friends in that way, pitting herself against them, but what choice did she have? They pushed her out of their circle a long time ago. Now, she would push back a little, show them the life she was living. Prove to them how much she had become her own person.

A tap on her door.

Derek moved closer to the door with his good hand on his sidearm.

Samantha waved for the young woman to enter.

"Hello, Miss Samantha, I'm Lisa, your new assistant." She seemed nervous and held onto her tablet with shifting hands.

Samantha leaned back in her chair and studied the woman, another early twenty-something woman, pretty and dressed in a sleek black suit. Samantha wanted to warn Lisa being near her would be a danger to her health. In one week, she'd gone through two assistants, one arrested and sent to who knows where and one killed by militants in a helicopter attack. She chuckled and shook her head. When thinking of it, it seemed so ridiculous. "Nice to meet you, Lisa. Derek, give her some room."

Derek backed away but kept his hand on his firearm.

"Please, come in."

Lisa timidly stepped toward her desk. "Here are the reports for France for you to go over."

"Send it to my station." Samantha pointed at her screen.

Lisa clutched her tablet against her chest. "We've been directed to deal in these tablets only, moving forward." She handed her the device.

"Thank you, I'll go over them and get back to you."

"Thank you and, Samantha? We're all very happy to have you back." The corners of her mouth pushed to the sides of her face and almost looked genuine.

Samantha paused on her eyes. The blue hue looked familiar, maybe she thought of Joey at first, but that wasn't it. This girl had an old feeling about her eyes, like she'd seen too much for a person of her age. Zach probably picked up another sorrow case, he seemed to have a soft spot for people without families and turbulent histories.

"Thanks, Lisa. If there is anything else, let me know."

With Lisa gone and Samantha's guard dog calmed down, she turned on the tablet. For the next few hours, she signed off on orders and directed air drops of the cure over designated spots across much of Europe and Asia. She wondered how much weight her signatures held and if she didn't sign off on one, would the drop not happen? She didn't want to test it.

With much of the formalities taken care of, she turned the TV on and changed to the news channel. The news reporter wore a red tie and his eyes looked puffy. He stared directly at the camera in silence. The silence brought her out of her chair and she stood in front of the TV. The man seemed to be frozen on screen. Finally he moved and looked to something off camera.

"You sure?" He faced the camera again with a smile spreading across his face. "We just got word from the White House that a deal has been made with the mysterious Zach Ryan Baker. Distribution of the cure shall commence immediately throughout the country."

Cheers roared in the offices of ZRB. Samantha saw Derek do a fist pump. She took another step closer to the TV and listened to the excited reporter talking about the LA and Preston drops and how the positive results were confirmed and real. It *was* a cure.

Zach did it. He got the US to agree to let him distribute unobstructed. She figured there was more to the deal than what was reported, but it didn't matter. Finally, she could save everyone in the country.

She sat back in her chair.

Lisa busted into the room, full of smiles. She skipped to the side of her desk.

What happened to knocking?

"Did you hear? We're distributing in America."

"Yeah, it's incredible. I'm really not sure why it took so long." She looked at the news reports discussing some of the statistics. Apparently, over ten million Americans had perished to the Cough and estimates were getting close to a billion worldwide as the poorer, crowded countries had been hit the worst.

With that many people sick, how could Zach make good on the promises he'd made? Samantha had already seen the documents showing much of their supply was heading to Europe and Asia. What was left for America?

"Oh, and Zach sent over the US details. Check your . . . tablet?" Lisa bit her lower lip.

Samantha skimmed the pages, seeing the towns and delivery estimates scroll by: Detroit, Chicago, New York, Miami, Barstow, Springfield, and many more. She saw her signature request on each delivery. She sighed and thought it was a waste of time to sign each page. Then she reached the bottom and a *Sign All* button appeared.

She pressed it and signed her name across the screen.

Done. The world could recover from this. Things could get back to normal and then she could have Zach all to herself. She thought about staying in his amazing cliffside house and resisted the urge to hug herself. Soon the world would know about their relationship and they'd be the power couple who'd saved them all. Maybe when things settled down they could go do an interview with Oprah. Did she still do interviews?

She felt the weight lifting off her shoulders. Everyone would have the cure in the next few days, there wasn't a need to fight anymore. Tapping the thin red line over her eye, she searched for a hint of pain, but it didn't come.

"Woo-hoo!" Lisa yelled.

Samantha jumped back in her seat and Derek stepped forward with his hand on his gun.

Lisa smiled and looked from her to Derek. "Sorry, but this is the best news ever. We should throw a floor party." Her eyes went big with enthusiasm.

While Samantha did agree about it being great news, she didn't share in her enthusiasm for a floor party, as that meant it would include the whole sixteenth floor—she didn't have many fans out there. "I don't—"

"No, Miss Samantha, we are doing this. After all you've been through, you need this. I'll make all the arrangements."

Samantha opened her mouth in protest but Lisa turned and left the office.

"Feisty one," Derek said.

"Yeah, she means well. I think."

"Good, you should always have some doubt about the people around you, especially new people."

Samantha looked past her glass door. Lisa stood next to the receptionist desk with her arms flailing in excitement. She seemed harmless, but she couldn't remember ever seeing her before. "I think there is room for trust in people."

"Don't let them fool you. If I dig, I can find out something dark on Lisa."

"Like what, she cheats on crossword puzzles?"

"You might be surprised what people suppress in public. I'm the closest thing in this world to a mind reader and people's minds are a terrifying place."

"Really, you think Lisa is a possible threat?"

"I don't know yet, but she faltered when saying tablet. It was strange."

"So?" Samantha rolled her eyes but had thought it was weird as well.

"Something is behind those eyes, way beyond the floor party planning, and there is a depth to them. I find her very interesting."

She opened her laptop and typed in Lisa. Her smiling face popped up but under employee information, it just said pending. She must have been a new hire and the HR department hadn't updated her info; unusual but nothing to send up red flags about. Now she wanted to know more about this Lisa and why Derek had an interest in her.

"Fine, let's make a bet then. You find your 'something dark' on Lisa and I won't complain about you shadowing me. On the other hand, if it isn't sufficiently dark, I win and you will call me Samantha and drop the Miss crap."

"Done, but I bet you won't like what I find."

Her phone dinged. A text.

Zach: They are lying. Launch protocol 32 from your station.

Samantha: What?

Zach: I'm pinned down right now. The whole meeting was a setup. They are trying to take it from us. Launch 32!

Samantha: I just signed all the releases for a US distribution, Lisa gave me the list.

Zach: Who's Lisa? 32 do it now! gtg omw

Samantha set her phone on the desk and scrambled to get her laptop open. She sent the mouse to the protocol box and scrolled down to thirty-two. Hesitating, she glanced through her glass wall at Lisa and shook her head. There she stood, holding the phone, probably ordering catering for the floor party. How did Zach not know who she was? He knew everyone.

Samantha pressed thirty-two and clicked on the confirmation. A metal shade slammed over the window behind her. Derek pushed off the wall and drew his gun. She leaned back in her chair and sighed. "I think I'm going to have to get used to you calling me Miss Samantha."

CHAPTER 16

"YOU THINK HE'S GOING TO be okay?" Hank asked, staring at the machine containing his dad.

"Yeah, he should be fine," Harris said.

"We have to do something about Earth, Harris."

"I know, and I've already set it up. We could leave now. Your dad is safe here and from the sound of it, Earth needs our help."

Hank nodded and they discussed a rough plan while walking to the Alius stone. He'd threatened Jack with a few choice words to drive home the importance of taking care of his dad in his absence.

"Can you ride a motorcycle?" Harris asked.

HANK'S BUTT FELT SORE FROM the long ride and he looked suspiciously at the large warehouse outside of Albuquerque, New Mexico. "So that's where they're making the cure?"

"Yes." Harris kneeled next to a fence and scanned the area. "Only a couple of guards. Shouldn't be hard to find out what's going on inside."

A nearby shed blocked them from the guards' line of sight. Barbed wire swirled over the top of the fence and a few blacked-out school buses were the only vehicles parked near the doors of the warehouse.

Their motorcycles were parked a few miles down the dirt road leading to the warehouse. They stuffed them behind a group of bushes and snuck up to the back of the building using the sparse vegetation as cover.

"So, how are we going to get in there?" Hank asked.

"I'm going to the back door, while you—"

Alarms blared out from speakers around the building.

They laid flat against the ground, turning their heads in every direction. Harris brought a gun out. "Something's wrong. I don't think that's for us," he whispered.

Hank's breath stirred up dust and he breathed it in with his panting. He wanted to cough it out but refused to make a sound. A guard ran around the building's corner and punched a code into a panel next to the door. He flung the door open and entered the building.

"They're on lockdown," Harris said and then froze. "Hear that?"

"No."

"Get up." He grabbed Hank by the arm, lifting him to his feet and pulling him away from the fence.

Hank stood, shocked at Harris's strength, before running with him. Harris slid into a ditch and lay on the bank. Hank matched him and looked around for the danger Harris was obviously sensing.

Harris rolled in the dirt. "Get dirty, they might not see us." Harris picked up handfuls and threw it over his clothes.

Hank rolled around, getting his clothes dirty.

Harris stopped and put a hand on him. "Do not move."

He heard it now. The sound grew and he searched the sky.

"There," Harris said.

Hank looked in the direction Harris was watching. A group of black helicopters flew toward them. He saw the details of the angled helicopters and the blacked out glass. He pressed his body against the dirt bank and tensed up.

"Stay still, they're going to fly right over us."

The helicopters roared overhead and reached the building. Two hovered, while one landed. Dust swirled around the one as men ran out of it.

Black rope lines dangled from the other two and soldiers dropped in quick succession. Hank counted a dozen soldiers on the roof with another six on the ground. The soldiers on the ground threw something on the door to the building and it stuck against it.

An explosion rocked the roof and the door at the same time. The soldiers on the roof dropped from sight, as four of the soldiers on the ground ran into the building. Two stayed in position, next to the door.

"What are they doing?" Hank searched for an American flag or any identifiers beyond the double triangle.

"Must be a militia of some sort. When you're the only person with a cure for the world's problems, you'll get all kinds of unwanted attention."

"They're fighting with us?"

"Don't mistake a common enemy with a friend. They'd shoot at you just the same as they would the people in that building." Harris peered over the desert grass. "I don't like this. Something's not right here."

Rapid gunfire blasted from inside the building. The two helicopters rose higher into the sky and hovered. More gunfire and an explosion, smoke billowed out from a hole in the roof. The soldiers guarding the outside rushed into the building. More gunfire and two more explosions. A few more scattered shots and then silence. The helicopters thumped away from above but not another sound of gunfire.

"Look!" Hank pointed at the door. A soldier staggered out of the door holding his chest. Blood spilled over his hand and he collapsed to the dirt near the door.

"We've got to help him."

"We step out there and we'll get shot, Hank. Stay here."

Hank balled up his fists and hammered the dirt in front of him. He heard a scream from inside the building. Jumping up before Harris could grab him, he made a run for the fence.

Harris yelled for him to stop, but he couldn't just sit by and watch the man die. Hank reached the fence and threw his jacket over the barbed wire. On his climb up, he felt a hand grasp his ankle. He kicked it off and lunged his body over the fence, striking the ground. He turned back to see Harris cutting a hole through the fence with a laser pen.

"Could have given me a second." Harris pushed the cut fence in and stepped through. He ducked next to the shed and Hank settled in behind him. Harris peeped around the corner and came back. "That guy's dead. Sorry, Hank."

"This may be our best way to get into that place," Hank said.

"This chaos has formed a nice distraction. We make a run for the building and we have a chance of not getting shot from above. How fast can you run?"

Hank shrugged. "I don't know, pretty fast I guess."

Harris nodded, looking like he'd expected a more precise answer. "Three, two, one."

The smell of smoke hit his nose as soon as they entered the door, and he thought of the burnt building in Ryjack. He remembered carrying Poly to the stone and getting her home. It felt so distant. A building in another world, a place he could escape. But this was Earth.

"Stay close," Harris whispered and pulled out two handguns.

Hank matched Harris step for step. They walked over a fallen soldier; his frozen, dead eyes looked shocked. Smoke wafted by and the light from the hole in the roof shone down on a cluster of dead soldiers. The long room was too wide for a hallway, with doors on one side. Each one marked with a number. Bullet holes riddled the walls, smears and splatters of blood caked every surface. But it wasn't just blood, there were splatters of black mixed in with the rest.

"Those aren't gunshot wounds." Harris looked at the dead men. "They have cameras on them."

Hank stared at the slice wounds on one of the soldiers and felt his anger rising. Slain like animals at a slaughter house.

The loud sound of the helicopter blades took off. Dust blew past the door and down the hole in the roof. Hank watched as the hovering helicopters flew away.

"Retreating," Harris explained, looking through the hole. "But I bet they'll be back. Let's get what we came for and get out of here."

Hank picked up a rifle off the concrete floor and pointed it at the doors down the hall. Whoever attacked the men, must have come from one of the doors.

Harris raised a hand, stopping to look at the ground. Hank looked around him to see what he was staring at. A long dagger with a curved blade and golden hilt stuck out of one of the soldiers. He knew that blade, seen it many times on another planet.

All of the doors to the hallway flung open and Arracks poured into the space. There was no rush to their movements as they slowly walked toward the two in a seemingly never ending supply. Many carried the long curved daggers in their hands.

Seeing their faces brought back a flood of horrible memories. Hank had watched their leaders die from the cloud that covered their planet. He swallowed and wondered if any of these Arracks were there that day. Would any of them recognize the delivery man?

Harris's back bumped into his. "Don't move."

Both stuffed their guns away and held up their hands. Hank glanced from one set of yellow eyes to the next. The idea of Arracks on Earth choked out any rational thought. As they got closer, some sniffed the air and cocked their heads at the visitors. Many hissed out words Hank didn't understand.

"I'm sorry, Hank," Harris whispered.

"Don't be, I got you into this mess," he replied.

"Maybe, but if they know who we are, we're both dead."

CHAPTER 17

IT'D BEEN TWO HOURS SINCE the announcement came across the radio. The US was getting the cure. Joey stared out the side window. Many people on the freeway had left their cars and now danced in the spaces between. Music blared and the whole freeway seemed to have turned into an impromptu party.

But not everyone was partying.

They also passed piles of dead bodies. People who had got the Cough early were cast out of their cars by the roving groups of people Lucas called the Death Squads.

Joey wanted to be happy for the cure, but wondered if they could truly come back from it all. He thought of the back room at the gas station and shook his head. He never thought his world could get close to the horrors of Ryjack, but in a brief moment, Earth had been transformed into a post-apocalyptic nightmare. Could a person come back from doing such atrocities? Could people forget what they saw and move on with a normal life? Based on watching people from the military come home from wars, he guessed some could and others couldn't, but everyone would be changed.

Lucas honked the horn and waved at people to get out of the way. Many people walked in between cars, giving them strange looks as they were one of the few cars going the opposite direction. They wanted to get out of the city while the rest of the country would be crowding into every major city, awaiting a shipment of the cure. Julie figured the traffic would lighten as they got away from the city; they had yet to see evidence of it.

The car's AC blew on Joey's face, but the noon sun blared down on his black shirt and he felt the heat. He blinked to moisten his eyes, watching a man wearing a face mask drag a body toward another small pile of bodies.

Marcus had killed them. And what made it worse was that he had her. He might even be with her right at that very moment. It dug deep that Samantha chose him over them. Could he really blame her? Joey would have been happy for her to find a man. At this point, he would've liked it if she'd rubbed it in his face, but she picked a man set on destroying their world.

Samantha fell for a man who had wrecked all their lives and killed their parents. It was painfully clear she didn't *see* that man; he saw the look in her eyes. She really cared for this Zach guy, and it blinded her to what she should be seeing.

He should have tried harder to include her back into the group. How could they be the Preston Six with one of them missing? The Preston Five didn't feel right. Even knowing

Hank was safe in Preston didn't help the fact they were separated. Joey didn't feel complete without Samantha in his life. He wanted her as his friend.

Poly touched his arm and offered a smile.

He placed a hand on hers in exchange. She refused to look out the windows, choosing to look at the floor or straight ahead. He thought it endearing she wasn't numb to it all, she still felt for those around her. Joey felt some of the shock wearing off as they drove by a dead child on the side of the road. Not long ago, it would have rocked their worlds to see such a horrible sight. Now, it didn't even make idle conversation. He wanted back his innocence, but life had other plans, and it played for keeps.

His hand shook in hers and she gave it a sharp glance. She couldn't get used to his shakes, no matter how much she tried to hide it. "I'm okay." He willed it to be a small shake and after a minute it stopped shaking all together.

"With this traffic, we'll be back in Preston a month from now." Lucas leaned back and sighed. "Get out of the way."

"Just chill," Julie said. "They should be happy, the cure is being delivered to the world."

"Should they? They have no idea who is delivering it to them."

Joey would have been happy as well, but Lucas was right, the person delivering it is what caused trepidation.

"I have an aunt in Miami, I hope she gets the cure," Poly said out loud to herself. She kept her attention on her hands in her lap.

"How many cures do we have left?" Julie asked.

"Eight," Poly said.

Julie popped the glove box and pulled out a cure box with the ZRB logo on it. "Let me see a vial."

Poly pulled one from her bag and handed it up. Julie opened the box and held the two vials in sunlight. The one from Vanar was clear, the one from ZRB had a yellow tint to it.

"Looks like urine," Lucas said.

"It's different," Julie mumbled to herself.

"Yeah, probably a different process or something," Poly said.

"What if it's a different cure?" Julie paused and set the vials on her lap. "If I had an analyzer attachment to my Pana..." She turned and looked back at Poly and Joey. "On the surface, it looks like he created this Cough and plans to swoop in as the hero of the world and cure it, right? I mean it's pretty obvious."

"Sort of like someone kicking you in the balls and expecting a thanks when they hand you a bag of ice," Lucas interjected.

Julie continued, "I feel there are other motivations at play here. Why change his appearance when we are the only people on the planet who would have any clue who he is? Why take on Samantha? Or is this Zach guy even Marcus? Could we be dealing with some psycho equivalent?"

"To mess with us," Lucas answered.

"Could it be so petty?" Poly asked. "I mean, look at us. We all jumped aboard, thinking this Zach guy was Marcus, and now, who knows. I agree with Julie, why do this whole production if so few people have any idea who you are?"

"Everything I read on Marcus told me how unpredictable he was; how he'd mastered the art of misdirection. He was able to clear the table of all competitors with his unorthodox tactics. Maybe he is planning something terrible for us. He may hate us in some very real way, but I doubt we are the bigger picture here. We might just be a heckler in the crowd, watching his grand opus."

"Yeah, but our blood saved him. Why would he be so spiteful to the people who saved him?" Joey asked and rubbed his arms.

"I've thought on that and what if we killed the one person he loved?"

Lucas coughed. "That thing was just a computer program."

"No, it was much more than that. He transported her entire consciousness into it. To Marcus, that program was his mother."

"And I killed her. . . ."

"A computer version of her, and I suspect he made a copy of her and brought it to Earth with him."

Lucas sighed. "She tried to kill me, I really didn't have a choice."

Joey perked up at the information. Lucas had never spoken of what happened in the bunker with Alice and he didn't appear to be adding any more to the mystery. He respected Lucas's privacy. Joey kept his own secret about Unitas. He couldn't even bring himself to discuss it with Poly.

"We should have killed him on the tarmac," Julie said.

"We aren't like that, Julie," Poly said.

"Really?" Julie asked.

"You haven't had to deal with killing someone. I've killed, Lucas has killed, Hank has killed, and Joey has killed . . . only you have the luxury of a clear conscious." Poly forced the words out, but it showed on her face she was holding much more back.

"*Clear?*" Julie turned around and looked at Poly in the backseat. "I've been in the same shit right next to you."

"You didn't have to stick a knife into a man's neck and have him cough blood on you—twice—now did you?" Poly was at a near scream. "Nor did you have to stare a man in the eyes while life left them."

Julie faced forward and crossed her arms.

Joey watched Poly glare at the back of Julie's head. He took her hand and shook his head. She pulled her hand away and looked out the window for the first time in a long time.

Lucas gave two light taps on the horn. A person slapped the hood of the car and then ran off into the stagnant traffic. "Where is Samantha?"

Julie unfolded her arms in a huff and pulled out her Pana. "She's still at ZRB headquarters." One of the few things they got out of the meeting with Samantha was her cell phone. Julie tagged it and now they could track her. Julie's fingers tapped the screen and she leaned in closer. Her face scrunched up in a mystery.

"What is it?" Poly asked. The malice had left her voice and Joey felt relieved. He hoped Poly and Julie's squabble wouldn't last.

"Something's strange. Her signal is very weak. I think something is trying to block the signal."

"Maybe they have an underground bunker or something?" Lucas said.

"No, it's more like a field around her, like a wave interrupter. It would kill almost any other signal but hers. Let me check their systems." She scrolled through her Panavice for what seemed like five minutes. "Something is very strange. They are in a total lockdown. Something called protocol thirty-two is running their systems now. I'm going to try and infiltrate it and see what's going on."

Lucas slowed the car down to a crawl as he anxiously watched Julie, barely sparing glances at the road.

Joey leaned forward and looked over her shoulder at the Panavice screen. She moved from page to page, clicking on certain boxes and typing in quick lines, before changing pages again. Watching it made him feel dizzy and he sat back down.

"I'm in."

Lucas didn't appear pleased about it. "Just be careful."

"Oh my god, they locked down all the cure factories. Many are reporting in . . . they are being attacked. Two have gone offline."

"What do you mean, they made a deal with the US?" Joey asked.

"I'm not sure, but someone out there obviously wants the cure for themselves. They must have found out where his factories were and tried to take them from him."

"Hello, Julie," a voice sounded from her Panavice.

Julie screeched and dropped it on her lap. Lucas went pale and slammed on the brake. Joey moved forward with Poly and peered at her screen.

A woman's face appeared, looking at each of them. She looked familiar to Joey. "My big sister told me about you," she said. "She had a finite amount of information she could share, but she gave me everything she knew about you. I found that interesting."

Julie covered her screen with her hand and mouthed the words. "She doesn't know about Vanar." She peeled her hand off the Panavice, revealing the woman's face. "Hello, Alice."

"Please, do not call me Alice. I am but a tiny replica. You can call me Renee. It was Alice's middle name."

"Does Marcus know you're talking with me?"

"Oh no, he would not approve. But I had to visit when I felt you touching me."

Lucas cringed and pushed himself against the door.

"Can you tell me what you are doing?" Julie asked.

"Protocol thirty-two has bestowed me with limited access to this world's internet. I am reacting to the threats poised to our different factories around the world. I am disabling the communications and creating various other problems for the people behind this offense."

Joey raised an eyebrow at all the information flowing from Renee.

"Thank you for your openness."

"I have a request."

Julie, with wide eyes looked at Lucas. "What is it?"

Lucas shook his head and made a hang up motion with his thumb and pinkie extended.

"We have found a use for Samantha and would like you to stop pursuing her. She is happy now."

"Samantha Roslin?" Julie verified.

"Yes."

"Why?"

"You are interfering with our plans. She is part of our long-term goals."

"We will not stop. We will never abandon her."

"I give you a seven percent chance of success. In fact, if you keep pushing, I give a ninety-three percent chance one or more of you will die."

"Your big sister gave me worse odds," Lucas said.

"What does that mean? I get from the inflection in your voice, you have more to say on this matter."

Lucas gritted his teeth and stared ahead.

"We don't know anything about Alice." Julie shook her head at Lucas. "Can I ask you a question about Marcus?"

"You can."

"Everything is pointing at Zach being Marcus, is Zach indeed Marcus?" A long pause. The screen switched back to the main screen. "She's gone." Julie sighed.

"What the hell was that about?" Lucas asked.

"I don't know. I *do* know this whole world just got a million times more dangerous. I should have been more careful. I should have known he'd bring part of her here."

"I thought I'd be rid of her," Lucas said.

"It's a small version of her former self. A whisper of what Alice was. You aren't facing what you faced in Vanar. But that doesn't mean we can ignore her either. With her in the systems and around the internet . . . it's going to be tough to mask our movements."

Lucas huffed and gripped both hands on the steering wheel, veering around a smoking car.

"I think we need help," Poly said.

"I agree and the first thing we need to do is," Julie held the ZRB cure up, "take this to Vanar and see if Harris can tell us what's different."

CHAPTER 18

AN ARRACK WITH A LAYERED necklace draping around its neck, stepped toward Hank and sniffed the air. "You're one of them. The Six." It hissed. "What are you doing here? Were you with them?" He pointed to the dead soldiers.

"No, we came to stop them," Hank said and looked at the floor. He didn't like lying.

"You smell familiar, who are you?" The Arrack looked at Harris.

Harris opened his mouth when an Arrack near him spoke up. "This . . ." he smelled the air and reeled back, "this is Harris Boone."

Hank closed his eyes and shook his head. The Arrack's cried out and rushed toward Harris.

"No!" The Arrack with the ornate necklace raised his sword. The horde stopped but sneered.

Hank watched Harris's hand twitching. He knew he wanted to pull his guns out and take out a dozen Arracks before they'd overwhelm him. Harris's unblinking, calculating stare took in each scowling face and Hank wondered if they had such an obvious advantage over him.

The head Arrack walked past Hank and close to Harris. "You are the human who tried to kill our entire species?" Spit flew from its mouth as it spoke. Its yellow eyes narrowed and it put a hand on its dagger.

"No, I had nothing to do with the letter."

It turned its attention to Hank, but Hank kept his eyes on the ground. "I heard the Six delivered the message. Were you there? Did you help kill so many of us?"

Hank glanced at Harris who gave him the tiniest shake of his head. Hank looked back at the ground. He'd watched the cloud pour from the envelope and spill onto the table as the Arracks breathed it in, choking to their deaths. He took part in it and he knew it would haunt him for the rest of his life. "Yes, I was there, but only to deliver a message of peace."

"*Peace*?" The thing hissed out between its sharp teeth. He spoke in his native tongue and the Arracks rumbled with a mixture of laughs and anger. "I would have prayed to Algo for five lifetimes just to get the luck of what has fallen in our hands today. We have the creator of the fog and the person who delivered it."

"Let the boy go and I won't give you any trouble," Harris said.

"Harris, I'm not leaving you."

"Neither of you are going anywhere! I didn't believe it, but *he* thought there was a chance you'd come to one of our centers. We have been given specific directions."

Hank stared at Harris when he felt the blade against his skin. He froze in place, nervous a single move would slice his own neck.

"Drop every weapon you have." The Arrack jerked on the dagger against Hank's neck.

Harris's eyes twitched and he put his hand on his gun. He saw the process in his mind, counting the Arracks and calculating his chance of survival. Hank hoped he was part of that equation. Wincing, he waited for an onslaught of bullets.

Harris dropped his gun to the floor, one at a time, followed by several knifes.

"Shuk," the Arrack with a necklace said.

They jumped on Harris and he fell to the ground. He disappeared under the pile and didn't so much as raise a hand to his attackers. Hank moved to stop them from hitting him, then felt a hit on the back of his head. The world spun and pain shot through his skull. He turned and grabbed the Arrack before it could hit him a second time with the butt of its dagger. It didn't weigh as much as he'd been expecting, was the last thought he had before they smothered him.

Receiving one more blow to the head, things became blurry.

Small silver hands restrained his body and lifted him up to his feet. They hauled him through a door, half carrying, half dragging him. Hank tried to pull away, but they had too many hands on him and the will had left his body. Looking up, he saw the long row of lights, illuminating the secret they were hiding below: Arracks were making the cure.

Arracks moved around, packaging the cure into cardboard boxes in an assembly line fashion. A few looked up from the line as he passed, but their faces swirled and his head pounded when he tried to focus on them. There had to be a thousand workers or more. How many cures did this place keep?

The factory view ended as they pushed him into a small room. They flopped his weak body onto a steel chair sitting in front of a steel pole rising into the ceiling. His arms were pulled behind his back and strapped to a pole. Moving to his feet, they tied them against the chair legs. He thought about the wheelchairs and the moment he'd seen his friends alive in that hospital hall. It had been a high point in his life. But here? No one even knew where he was. No one was going to save him.

He decided to face the Arracks eye to eye. The fluorescent lights above amplified his blurred vision, yet he saw the hate in their eyes as they circled around Harris. They were strapping him to a chair in front of him, tying him off to a metal sink at the edge of the room.

The Arracks left the room.

Hank's head ached and he tried to keep himself from slumping forward. Harris didn't appear to have the same control as his chin rested on his chest. His eyes were closed and blood dripped from his nose.

Hank sighed and stared at Harris's profile. He kicked his chair and tried to get Harris's attention. "Harris."

He stirred and jolted upright, taking in his surroundings with fire in his eyes. After a moment, the strain set in and he glanced at Hank. "You all right?"

"Head hurts like hell, but yeah."

The Arrack with the large necklace walked in the room. "He will be here soon."

"Who?" Hank asked.

The Arracks chuckled and hissed out a laugh. "Zach."

"Don't you mean Marcus?"

The Arrack got close to Hank's face. "I know who I mean, do you?" His breath reeked of decay, as if it hadn't brushed its teeth in a year.

The thing moved away from Hank and leaned close to Harris, smelling his shirt and strands of hair dangling over his brow. It blew out from his nose, pushing Harris's bangs back and leaving tiny droplets of moisture across his forehead. The creature then reared back and slapped Harris across the face. The sound cracked like a well-placed high five.

Harris reeled from the impact, his face quickly changing to rage. "Is that all you've got?" Spittle flew from his mouth and the veins in his neck and forehead bulged. Hank backed away from the display.

At the open door to the room stood another Arrack, waiting at the threshold and watching the display. The necklace Arrack motioned for the next Arrack. It jumped over to Harris, closed its fist and hit Harris in the face.

"Is that *all*?" Harris raged.

Another Arrack stood at the door and waited as the last one left. The necklace Arrack motioned for him to come in. It was quick to pull out its dagger.

"You don't have the guts," Harris said, glaring at its curved blade.

The creature struck Harris in the shoulder with it, slicing through his shirt and into the meaty part of his muscle.

Harris laughed and sucked in a quick burst of air and then spit blood all over the face of the Arrack with the dagger. It swung its dagger at Harris's neck.

"Stop!" Necklace Arrack demanded. "He does not get a quick death, there are many in line behind you. We shall all get a turn."

The Arrack pulled back its dagger and licked the blood off the blade.

"You're still taking orders from him?" Harris yelled. "You should get the privilege of killing me. I killed your entire planet." He laughed. "If you let me live, I'll do it again."

The Arracks grumbled as the necklace Arrack translated what he said.

Hank tried to look past the maniac sitting in front of him. He didn't know this man. Harris was always cool under pressure, he wasn't the type to crack. "Harris, what are you doing?" he whispered, as the murmuring of Arracks became a torrent of shouts and cries.

In between Arracks, Harris said, "I'll keep them off you, best I can."

Hank looked at the Arracks lining up in the room and out the window, where he could see the line reaching the far wall of the warehouse. The next Arrack punched Harris in the stomach and then started choking him until another Arrack pushed it out of the way.

Harris laughed and coughed. The man was taking it for him. "Bring on the next one!"

This one punched Harris in the face.

Hank, too horrified to watch, saw the feet shuffle forward and listened to the thumps and the crazy rants coming from

Harris. Over time, the rants slowed and became weak, but the Arracks didn't stop. A fresh Arrack followed the next, until he no longer heard a noise from Harris, only the soft thumps from punches and kicks.

"Stop it! You're going to kill him," Hank pleaded.

They ignored him.

Harris sat limp, and maybe he had already died and they were beating his dead body. Hank sucked in his lip and looked to the ceiling. He felt tears building and wished for somebody or something to help them. He struggled against his straps for the hundredth time, forcing them further into his wrists.

Harris's ploy had been to draw all their hate to him and it seemed to work, but as the next Arrack slammed the butt of his dagger against Harris's fingers, Hank knew they were not touching him for a reason. Marcus must have instructed them not to injure him. If Harris wanted this beating over what Marcus brought . . . Hank had more to worry about than being beaten within an inch of his life.

CHAPTER 19

SAMANTHA LOOKED OVER THE TOP of her desk at the employees scurrying around in a panic over the total shutdown. The elevators didn't work, the windows were blocked, the exits locked, and even her cell phone stopped working. The building had effectively shut itself off from the world.

Derek held out his gun and watched the glass door, expecting an intruder at any second. She might have told him to calm down, but she needed him on high alert. Something had gone terribly wrong after the White House meeting. Her heart raced as she thought about Zach's situation.

"I think we should get you out of this area. It's too hard to secure if there's an attack." Derek spared a second to give her a look of seriousness.

"No, not yet." She glanced at the TV and the president had come on screen. She turned up the volume.

"America, I come to you at the most egregious of times. We are faced with the worst epidemic in the modern world. We are mourning our friends and relatives at an alarming rate." He grasped his podium with both hands and stared into the camera. Samantha knew the look, he was pissed.

"But we are not without hope. A single company, a single man, has produced a cure and a vaccine. But the price he's asked for compliance is too much for any American to bear in the long term. We have declared Zach Ryan Baker an enemy of the state for crimes against the United States of America. The employees of ZRB have until midnight, Pacific Standard Time, to clear from the buildings they work in and cut all ties with ZRB. Any failure to do so will result in criminal charges. We are in the process of confiscating all of ZRB's cures to properly distribute them to the United States and the rest of the world—without conditions, without costs, without any reason, but it being the right thing to do."

Samantha covered her open mouth as she stared at the screen, then she felt the small scar above her eye. Zach was a criminal now, an enemy of the state. Her own government had turned against them. All she and Zach wanted to do was cure the world. How could they be so cruel? The world needed the cure and they needed it *now*. Why was everyone trying to stop them from delivering it?

The screen flickered and Zach's smiling face appeared on the screen. The grainy picture was up close and shook as if he was holding the camera out in front of himself.

"Hello, America." He waved to the camera and showed his bright white teeth. "I'm the single man with the cure, the head of the single company creating it. What the President of the United States isn't saying is who he is taking orders from. Not the American people, but a small group of men bound on stopping me at any cost in order to control this disease. But I haven't and won't let that happen, even on an erroneous presidential order. Even as I speak, these men are attacking my factories, not with US soldiers but with mercenaries. If this was about getting you the cure, then why attack the very factories making it? We were able to deter most of these attacks, but sadly some were lost. South Africa, Vietnam, and Australia, those were your shipments. They will be delayed because of your weakness in letting these men dictate your actions, Mr. President.

"We are at the edge of no return, but with this cure we have a way back—if we hurry. I ask the president, the men behind the president, and all other leaders to not impede my distribution of the cure. And to prove my intentions are only to get the cure to as many as possible, I am sending out teams of trucks to every major city in America over the next twenty-four hours."

He leaned in closer to the camera. "America . . . if you don't receive the cure, it is only a result of your president physically stopping my trucks. And just to keep everything real public, I have attached a web cam to every heavily-armed caravan. You can watch the trucks as they travel to each destination, and the live feeds will be available on our company's website. Mr. President, do you really want to stop the cure from reaching your citizens? Let the trucks roll."

Samantha breathed out, not realizing she had been holding her breath.

The screen went black.

"Zach just put it in the public's hands," Derek said. "The president will have a hell of a time trying to convince everyone now."

Samantha had seen the papers, the schedules for the trucks. The trucks would be rolling out within the hour and the whole world would be watching to make sure they got there. Zach was a genius. She didn't know how he'd hacked into the TV stream, but she couldn't figure out half the things he accomplished.

In the next few days, the world would have the cure they were waiting for and the recovery could start. They could finally tell their story to the world and the president would have to pardon Zach and anyone involved with ZRB. How could they arrest them for saving the world? What jury would convict them?

The glass door pushed opened. Lisa stepped in and found herself staring at the end of Derek's gun. She didn't flinch and gave Derek a glare. "Really?" Lisa said and put her hand on her hip. Derek lowered his gun and took a step back. "Thank you." She walked toward Samantha.

"What is it, Lisa?"

"They're kind of going crazy out there. Many want to leave, but the doors are locked. I think you have the only access to open them." Lisa let the unasked question hang in the air.

"We are just about to send out shipments across the whole world and they want to leave?" Samantha felt anger building. She wanted to go out and slap some sense into the people out there. There was no way she was letting them leave.

"They're scared. I mean, the president just told them to leave."

"No. No one is leaving until we make sure all shipments have made it to their respective destinations. I want those webcams working and everything else to go without a hitch." Samantha tried to leave no room for argument in her voice.

Lisa cocked her head and smiled. "I guess this means no more floor party? I'll have to call the pizza guy off."

"You don't mind staying?" Samantha asked.

"Please, you'd have to drag me out of here."

"Good, now get out there and tell everyone to get back to work," Samantha demanded.

Lisa's eyes narrowed and Samantha thought she saw a hint of anger before she smoothed it out. "As you say, Miss Samantha."

The power to the whole building shut off. A few people on the floor let out screams.

Samantha sighed and looked at the ceiling. She wondered if the power was manually shut off or they had truly lost power.

"We should move," Derek said. "If it is the start of an attack, this office will be the first place they come."

An attack? Samantha walked around her desk and wished she looked half as calm as Lisa. Protocol should have secured the building, but how secure? She didn't want to find out. "Where should we go?"

"There's a safe room on. . . ." he glanced at Lisa, "I'll just take you there."

Lisa rolled her eyes. "I'm supposed to stay with Samantha. Zach texted me not long ago." She held out her phone.

"*Miss* Samantha..." Derek muttered.

Samantha took her phone and inspected the text. It was from Zach. "Fine." She handed Lisa back the phone.

"Thank you," Lisa said.

"It's on the first floor, hope you ladies are wearing your walking heels today."

Samantha followed Derek, with Lisa taking up the rear. People congregated near the receptionist's desk and silence fell as they saw her nearing. All eyes were on her.

If she told them she was going to open the doors, the whole group would come with her. If an attack happened, it would be disastrous to have a meatball of people in one spot. "We have suspicions the power may have been shut off. We are going down to check the perimeter and once we establish an all clear, we'll let you know." Derek had formed the cover story and Samantha was grateful.

"You can't just leave us here!"

"Yeah, it's against the law or something to lock us in like this."

Samantha held up her hands and called for silence. "Listen, we are only trying to keep everyone safe. No one will be held here. But I need to follow all safety protocols before we can open the doors. Don't you all remember the assault on the front lawn?"

They murmured in agreement. *Good.* With shoulders back, she marched toward the staircase, keeping her eyes forward. She pushed the fire emergency exit door open and stood on the landing of the staircase. Derek followed right behind her while Lisa hugged his heels. The number sixteen door closed and Samantha glanced at the two people standing with her. "Where to?"

Derek nodded his head and brought out his gun. Samantha followed him down the stairs. Fifteen, fourteen, but on the next landing, there was no door. She paused and Derek must have noticed the clicking of her heels had stopped. He turned around and raised an eyebrow.

"There should be a door here."

"Floor thirteen." Derek shrugged.

"Yeah, I know it isn't on the elevator, but I believed it was a superstitious thing. I never thought there was actually a hidden floor in the building."

Lisa's eyes narrowed and she stared at the wall where a door should have been. She brushed her hand over the wall and right when Samantha was about to ask her what she was doing, a screen lit up from behind the wall.

With wide eyes, Samantha moved closer to the screen. "It's a keypad." The numbers ran like a ten key on the screen.

"Do you know the code?" Lisa asked.

"I don't think we should be messing with this stuff," Derek said.

"There is some freaking secret floor I didn't know about." She hated admitting she didn't know about it. "Don't you think this would be the most secure floor to be in?"

Derek holstered his gun and sighed. "You're probably right."

Samantha turned back to the screen and typed in her access code to get into the computer files. The panel went dark and she stepped back, wondering if she put in the wrong code. Maybe it took a while to reset. She could use her employee number, or...

Samantha gasped as the entire wall slid open like a bank vault. Derek brought out his gun. She felt his nervous energy. Turning to Lisa, she saw her tilting her head, trying to see into the room as the door slowly opened. She didn't seem nervous at all; she seemed excited about it.

The door clicked when fully open and the room beyond didn't look much different than the computer tech room she'd seen on the lower floors. A person with a hoodie pulled over their head ran to the back of the long room and out through a door.

"Hey," Derek called out, but the person never looked back.

Samantha stepped into the room with Lisa and Derek on either side of her. The unmanned computer stations displayed surveillance feeds. The first few showed multiple views of headquarters. Many more showed locations she wasn't familiar with. They looked like parking lots or the insides of empty warehouses. Some were shrouded in the darkness of night. But it wasn't night anywhere in America . . . the night shots must have been on another continent.

Her brow furrowed. Zach should have told her about this mass surveillance. She understood they needed to protect their assets, but as the Vice President of the company, she should know these kinds of things. It sent a pain in her gut and she wondered what else he hadn't told her. How many secret floors did he hide from her?

She froze in front of a set of monitors. She knew this place. Zach's house. The outside, front door, and kitchen were displayed on three screens, but she didn't care about any of those. Shocked, she stared at the fourth and felt the color leaving her face. She took notice of the crumpled bed sheets, the exact way she left them this morning. Had someone watched them? Was there a recording? She had trouble standing and leaned against the desk.

"You know that house?" Derek glanced at the screen before returning to his manic scan of the floor.

"No." She moved away from the screen. Later, if she could get alone, she'd destroy those computers and whatever content they held.

Lisa scurried around the place, typing into a computer here or there before moving onto the next, never looking up at them.

"What are you doing?" Samantha asked, thinking she'd opened a door that maybe Lisa shouldn't have seen. If the VP wasn't told about this floor, should the VP's assistant know?

"How much do you guys really know about Zach?" Lisa asked.

Anger quickly filled Samantha, she was sick of the question and she scowled.

Lisa rolled her eyes at the look and went to the next computer. "If you think you know who Zach is, I think you should look at this, *Miss* Samantha." Lisa's voice changed to one full of contempt and arrogance.

Samantha walked toward this different Lisa, stopping short to glance at the ceiling. A hissing sound, like air escaping from a tire, came from above. A cloud of white mist shot out of pipes across the whole ceiling. The mist flowed around her and she felt a stiff hand grabbing her arm.

Derek pulled her toward the door, but she knew it was too late. She felt the mist entering with each breath. His grip lessened as he fell to his knees.

"I'm sorry," he said before he collapsed.

There had to be an error. This couldn't be happening to her. Not in her own house. Samantha lost control of her muscles and collapsed to the floor.

CHAPTER 20

POLY FIDGETED WITH THE THROWING knife at her hip. They were finally at the stone in Watchers Woods and she was filled with trepidation. Looking to Lucas, who knelt next to the stone with a stoic expression, she saw he felt the same way. She trusted him to get them to the right destination, but she couldn't shake the feeling they would end up somewhere horrible every time they used a stone.

Just get on with it, Poly wanted to say, but kept back and stopped her pacing. If by chance they were sent to Ryjack or some other horrible world, she'd be ready. Joey took her hand and held it. She liked the contact, even though it might slow her reaction time down by a split second. She wanted more contact from him.

Ever since they'd found out who Samantha was involved with, he felt distant. She saw the strain on his face growing with each discovery of how deep into it she was. Poly loved Samantha and she was sure he loved her as well, as a friend. She tamped down her insecurities. Joey loved her the way a man loves a woman. They were more than friends. They shared a connection she didn't plan on sharing with another person for the rest of her life.

A twitch resonated from his hand. She firmed up her grip and gave him a smile. He'd saved them all with the sacrifice of his own body. She hated when he did it—he could have died—but she loved how he'd risked everything to save his friends, to save her. He was the true definition of a hero. However, she made him promise to never do it again. She preferred to have her hero by her side, not six feet under.

"Here we go." Lucas typed in the code.

The humming started and she sucked in a breath, grasping a throwing knife with her free hand. Harris's house flipped into existence. The succulent forest air changed to crisp, recycled air. Guns pointed in their direction until the guards saw who they were.

Jack ran up to them. "Hey, Julie, guys, so glad to see you."

"Hey, Jack. Is Harris here?" Julie asked.

Jack frowned. "He's not with you? He left with Hank a couple days ago. Trip's still recovering in the medical wing."

"What happened to Trip?" Lucas rushed to Jack.

"He was shot and in pretty bad shape. Hank brought him here for medical attention. Good thing he did too, because the doctors said they had a tough time saving his life. You all aren't as genetically strong as—"

"Jack," Joey interrupted. "What were Harris and Hank doing? Where are they?"

"They went to stop Marcus."

Poly breathed deep and squeezed Joey's hand. She hadn't wanted to leave Hank behind when he was sick. She'd wanted to take him with them. They should have found a van or something; they could have found a bed for him to recover in.

"On *Earth*?" Julie asked, shaking her head. "No, that's not possible, I would have known. His Pana would have shown up." She wiggled her Panavice in the air.

"He left all that stuff behind, said Marcus could track him if he brought it. You know Marcus can track yours, right?"

"I'd like to see him try. I rewrote the whole tracker code on mine and I doubt he'd be able to see me."

"Really? I'd love to see what code you—"

"Guys," Lucas butted in, "sorry to interrupt the nerd convention here, but we came for a reason."

Julie cleared her throat and glanced at Lucas with a hint of annoyance. "Marcus or Zach or ZRB, whoever they are, created a new cure for the Cough." She held the vial with a yellow tint to it. "The one we collected from you guys is this one." She held up a vial of clear liquid.

Jack's eyes narrowed. "I'm sorry, we don't have the analysis equipment here to verify the contents."

Julie sighed. "Who does?"

Jack rubbed his chin. "The only person who'd have access to that type of machinery would be President Denail."

"Travis?"

"Yes."

"Thanks, Jack. Lucas can you get us to Travis's stone?"

"Yep, I don't know why we don't just start going straight to Travis."

"Before you guys go," Jack held up a hand, "I wanted to let you know how much Vanar appreciates your involvement in our revolution and recovery. We are a long way from a fully functioning society, but we'd be nothing without you guys."

Poly had heard a variation of this same speech from many citizens of Vanar over the past few months. The Six were looked upon as the heroes who'd brought them back from the brink of disaster. She wasn't sure she agreed with their assessment, but always nodded and smiled, saying thank you. She felt like a liar. "Thanks, Jack."

After a round of goodbyes, Lucas knelt next to the stone and Poly braced for another jump. "Here we go."

The room flipped and they were in Travis's underground dome. They made their way down the hallway to the elevator, when a green light lit up and the doors slid open.

Travis appeared, with a big smile and arms spread out. Rushing over to them, he zeroed in on Poly first and wrapped her in a big, lingering hug. Then he shook hands with the boys and side-hugged Julie. His bright smile was infectious and Poly already felt brighter being around him. "So good to see you guys. You are like the light at the end of a dark tunnel."

"Good to be back," Poly said.

"Travis, we have something we were hoping you could look at." Julie held the two vials up.

Travis frowned and plucked the vials from Julie's hand. "The cures are different, aren't they?"

"Yes," Julie confirmed.

"Come on, we can take them to the lab and see what he's doing." Travis took Julie by the arm and led her toward the elevator.

Lucas adjusted his bow and followed. Poly stuck back with Joey and they filled the elevator.

Heading past the receptionist desk, Poly felt excited to see Gladius again; but when they arrived, a young man in a red suit looked up at them. She recognized the man instantly, it was Douglas.

"Douglas, can you make sure to cancel all my meetings for the day?" Travis asked.

"*All* of them?" he whined and rolled his eyes. "Fine, but if they get bitchy with me, I'm hanging up on them. I don't care if they're the mayor of whatever town."

"Thanks, Douglas."

Travis turned to the elevator, but Poly stepped toward Douglas. "Where's Gladius?"

"She's out on vacation or something," Douglas said.

She had come to know Gladius fairly well and while her initial impression of her was a shallow, selfish, rich girl, she'd changed her mind over time and found her to be a workaholic, and dedicated to her father like no one else. There was no way she'd be taking a vacation.

Douglas typed into his Panavice, not looking up.

Poly turned her attention to Travis. "She wouldn't take a vacation, where is she? Is she okay?"

Travis sighed and some of the early glow he held left his face. "Come on, we can talk more in the elevator." They crowded into the regular elevator and Travis typed into the panel. He leaned against the mirrored wall.

"Well?" Poly prompted.

"She thought she owed it to you guys to help in any way she could—we all feel that way—but she wanted to help in a more direct way."

"What does that mean?"

"She went to Earth and as far as I know, she's infiltrated ZRB's headquarters and is working to dismantle them from the inside."

Julie gasped.

Lucas smiled. "Hell yeah, that's awesome."

"No it's not," Poly said. "She could be killed, or who knows what."

Travis flinched at her words. "She knew the risks, and as much as I wanted her to stay here with me, I couldn't deny her sense of duty."

"No, tell her to come back, tell her to leave. Call her right now."

"I can't. I have no way to contact her."

Poly fumed and paced in the available space of the cramped elevator.

"We'll do everything we can to make sure she is safe when we get back to Earth," Joey said.

"Thank you."

The elevator stopped and the doors slid open. Poly looked around the room for any threats, a habit she had developed after being surprised one too many times. Joey did the same and covered the area where she wasn't looking. It made her smile when they instinctively worked so well together. The deep connection felt powerful, like they could overcome anything.

"Gary," Travis held out the two vials, "I want you to run a full analysis on these."

Gary wore a white coat with two beakers embroidered on his front pocket. He looked at the vials. "No problem, when do you need this done?"

"Now."

"But we are running a few tests on the air quality around Capital."

"Shut them down, this is more important."

Gary lowered his head. "Yes, Mr. President."

Poly couldn't get used to thinking of Travis as the president, let alone people calling him that. She hoped he never expected *her* to call him by his title. He was the same person as before, but she was lying to herself a bit in thinking that way. He seemed aged somehow. It was impossible, but he seemed to have a crease near his eyes, and his eyes now carried a certain weight to them. She wondered how the rebuilding of Vanar was really going.

Gary opened one of the vials and pulled some of the liquid out with a syringe and injected it into a square metal box. He twisted the lid shut and pushed a button. His computer screen danced with information. Julie leaned in close, but it might as well have been a foreign language to Poly.

She gazed around the room and the people occupying it. Many had stopped what they were doing and talked in small clusters, looking at them. She sighed and knew they recognized her. They probably wanted selfies to put on their walls and build up their social points. She didn't mind interacting, she enjoyed that part, but it wasn't her planet. Each time she interacted with someone here, she left a larger and larger footprint. She felt dirty, as if she was polluting their world with lies. Back on Earth, she could simply be Poly.

"Okay, all done," Gary said. "This is the cure to the cough, but they used a different protein, a more primitive type, like we would have used a few hundred years ago. It will still work but takes on a different color."

"So it's exactly the same?" Julie clarified.

"I didn't say that. There is also something registering on the biomechanical spectrum." Gary pushed his chair back and spun around. He took another syringe full of the vial and dropped it in a larger metal box. He sealed the top with a twist cap and pushed a button.

"You think there's a nanobot in it?" Travis said, looking at the machine humming.

"I don't know, we will find out in a minute. Why are you looking at this old stuff anyway? Is there another cough developing?"

"No," Travis stomped on the comment.

Gary shrugged and watched the computer screen blaze with numbers and letters. It stopped and he typed into it and then touched the screen, scrolling through different windows until an insect looking cylinder with spikes wrapping around its body appeared.

"There's your nanobot—tough to spot."

"Nanobot?" Julie leaned closer to the screen.

Poly frowned at the image. It freaked her out, thinking of some little thing like that roaming around in her body. Elation washed over her as she realized all of them had taken the clean cure from Vanar. They didn't have whatever it was in them, but the rest of world did, or was about to.

"What does it do?" Travis asked as he rubbed his eye in frustration.

"I don't know." Gary shrugged.

"Can you take a guess? It appears to have the structure of a neuron bot."

"I would agree, it does something in the brain, but unless it's activated, well . . . we won't know."

"Can you activate it?" Travis asked and Gary shook his head. He sighed.

"But if I had to guess, I'd say this is something nasty. The spikes on the side could be used for cutting, while the almost imperceptible tails have a fibrous surface, ideal for attaching inconspicuously to neurons. They could even control thoughts or at the least, give nudges. Or they could kill you."

Poly put her hand on her chest and looked at Joey. "We need to go and warn everyone." She wanted to run back to the stone.

"Yeah, let's get you guys back."

On the elevator rides back to the stone, they told Travis about the cure, how this Zach guy must be Marcus, and how he was distributing the cure worldwide. Travis took in the information with a grim expression. "You know, I don't think he has any intention of hurting you six. From everything I have learned, he has looked to keep you alive."

"Yeah, but now he has our blood and whatever else he took from us," Joey said.

"He didn't get everything from you," Travis reminded him.

"He's right, I still have both testicles." Lucas grabbed at his crotch.

"Ugh, Lucas, *no*." Julie put a hand over her face.

Travis laughed. "He's actually not far off. Marcus's ultimate goal was one of your children. Thought it could be the next step in human evolution. We even found some old documents where he'd referred to your spawn as the last chance for Vanar."

"What does that mean?"

"I have no idea, but we better hope Marcus isn't around to witness the birth of one of your kids."

Poly felt queasy and put her hand on her stomach. The elevator opened and they walked down the hall to the stone room in silence.

Travis turned to face them. "I need to apologize to each of you and Hank. If I live another thousand years, I'll never stop regretting what happened, what I did to each of you."

Poly shook her head. "You don't need to—"

"Yes, I do. And so much more. Especially to you, Poly, my dear. I almost killed you and then watched you nearly lose your life to Max. I should have acted sooner. I should have done more and now he's found a new place to call home on your planet. We thought we might have a hundred years before he got his claws into Earth. Harris and I believed we'd have time to concentrate on rebuilding our world. We were fools and that is just one of the reasons Gladius is so much of a better person than me. She had the courage to take action and help your world."

Poly watched the man tremble and couldn't find the words to soothe him. She grasped his hand and squeezed.

"I will make this right." Travis nodded, as if making a deal with himself. "Know you have the support of Vanar."

"Thanks, Travis," Poly said, letting his hand go after one more squeeze.

They didn't talk much as he said his goodbyes and walked down the hall. Poly had a sinking feeling she may never see Travis again. She had no reason to think it, but it weighed on her. They had shared a kiss, mostly Travis kissing her, but it was there. He knew about her and Joey and when he thought she wasn't looking, she'd spotted him sizing up Joey as if trying to understand what she was doing with him.

Joey gave hints that he saw something in the way Travis was with her, but Poly never mentioned the kiss. She'd rectify that as soon as they were alone. She didn't want to keep one thing from Joey. She wanted him to have her entirely.

"Come on," Joey said. He took her hand and guided her into the stone room.

Travis held a hand up and stared at her as they walked by, words paused on his lips and maybe he was feeling the same macabre feeling, but he kept his words to himself and watched them enter the dome.

Lucas didn't waste time and typed into the stone. "Here we go."

The smells of the forest washed over them and Poly took in the warm breeze.

"We need to tell everyone what they are taking. We have to warn someone at the top about this cure," Joey said.

"Why?" Julie asked.

"We should just put it on the internet or something," Lucas suggested.

"Yeah, 'cause conspiracy theories will stop people from curing themselves and their loved ones." Julie crossed her arms. "Don't you guys get it? It won't matter what we tell them, they still will take the cure. What is the alternative?"

Poly held her tongue because she had the exact thoughts as Julie. It was silly to even think they could stop the world from taking the cure. That nanobot would be in every person on the planet in the matter of a week and the only alternative was to die.

"Then what, we just give up and let him have Earth?" Joey asked.

This question brought on a long silence. Poly searched for the answer but there wasn't an easy path. That was Marcus's design, she was sure, he didn't want anyone to have a real choice in the matter. Maybe if Vanar wasn't in shambles, they could create a competing cure.

Joey ran his hands through his hair. "I think we need to go back to square one and do the one thing we can control."

"And what's that?" Julie asked.

"Get Samantha back."

"I'm driving!" Lucas blurted.

CHAPTER 21

THE BEATING HAD ENDED, EITHER everyone in line had a turn or they grew tired of thrashing an unconscious man. Hank wrestled against his constraints, and with each pull, the thin cords dug into his wrists.

The Arrack with the large necklace, walked into the room.

"He's dying," Hank pleaded, "we need to get him help!"

Harris hadn't moved in a while. Blood dripped from his nose and mouth. Cuts on the sides of his face had coagulated shut and were swelling.

The Arrack regarded him with a blank expression and walked behind Harris with a knife. Hank figured it was the end for Harris and after that, they would off him. He didn't want to watch Harris's last moments, choosing instead to face away.

Harris fell to the floor at his feet. Hank searched for any new wounds, but nothing. The cut straps dangled from his feet and hands. Turning back, he saw the Arrack approaching him with a dagger.

"I'm going to cut you loose, give me a reason to kill you, please," the Arrack hissed.

Hank stilled himself. He felt the Arrack's cold hands touching his legs and cutting the straps. The wrists were next and Hank felt blood rush back into his freed hands. He bounded to Harris on the floor and touched his hand. Still warm.

"He needs help," Hank pleaded with the Arrack.

"He won't get it, and doesn't deserve it. If I had my way, this would be a weekly thing. I'd heal him, just to where he'd be able to hurt again. The lines of Arracks would wrap around the world to get their fists on him."

The Arrack kicked Harris in the back and walked to the door. Harris coughed and opened his eyes. He groaned and blinked.

"He will be here soon." The Arrack left and locked the door.

Hank ignored the comment and rolled Harris onto his back.

Harris coughed and moved back to his side. He spat blood on the floor. "In my pocket, there is a white pill, get it out for me."

Hank searched in his jacket pocket and found a pill. He pulled it out and looked at the white pill between his fingers.

Harris eyed it and licked the blood on his lips. "Put it in my mouth."

Hank moved the pill close to Harris's mouth when he stopped. "What does it do?"

"It kills me, there's another in my pocket for you."

Hank jerked his hand back and set the pill on the chair. "I'm not killing you."

"Just put it on the floor, I can suck it into my mouth."

"No."

"Hank, we don't have time. Marcus will be here soon. He will use us to get to everyone else. He will play games with us like a cat might a mouse. Do you want to be the piece of a puzzle in his game? We can end it now before he has a chance." Harris coughed and spit another glob of blood on the floor. "Give me that pill. And I think you should take the second one."

"We are not giving up." Hank grabbed hold of Harris and lifted him up to a sitting position with his back resting against the chair. Hank tossed the pill away and heard it bouncing across the concrete floor.

Harris sighed. "It's not giving up. It's not giving him what he wants." Harris's eyes watered. "I've seen what he does with his enemies and it's a fate far worse than death."

"I am not going to let you die. We can take on Marcus, the two of us."

Harris laughed and coughed. "Listen, I deserve to die. How many Arracks did I kill? I destroyed their world. I knew what was in the envelope the whole time because I put it there. I had to destroy them before they destroyed us. Now tell me I don't deserve to be dead. Get me that pill."

Hank leaned back from Harris and fell on his butt. "You knew? I thought you were just talking back there. You killed them all?"

"Yes, and I'd do it again if it meant saving my world."

Hank reeled back further. He wasn't sure he knew the man sitting in front of him. He didn't have any love for the Arracks, but they were a people, they had a culture, they had children and friends.

"We would have died if not for Joey. You sent us to our deaths?"

"Yes, of course I did. Now get the second pill from my pocket. Even half a pill is more than enough to kill us both. Hank, you don't want to be the one to give up your friends to Marcus, do you? He will use us like bait, only after we've spilled everything we know. "

"This is crazy, I don't believe you." Spit flew from Hank's mouth as he moved toward Harris.

"Just give me the pill." Harris moved his mangled hand toward his pocket.

Hank slapped his hand away and yanked the second pill out of his jacket and threw it across the room.

Harris slumped. "It was worth a try. Don't listen to a thing he tells you. It will all be lies."

"You didn't really kill those Arracks, did you?"

"It doesn't matter now. Much like the Arracks, we've just been turned into pawns in Marcus's game."

Hank reached down and touched Harris's shoulder. He winced and Hank pulled back.

"This is an emotional gathering."

Hank turned to see a man standing at the door. He had expected Marcus, but this was someone else. "Who are you?"

"I'm Zach Baker. I own this building."

Harris coughed and squinted at Zach. "Is that Marcus?"

"You're not going to try anything are you, big man?" Zach asked, ignoring Harris's statement.

"You're that guy . . . the president of ZRB," Hank said and Zach bowed. "You're supposed to be Marcus. You're not him."

"I think you need to tell your friends this." Zach sidestepped him, getting closer to Harris.

Harris coughed and watched with swollen eyes as Zach moved across the room. He blinked and spit more blood on the floor. His right hand moved toward his jacket. Probably an instinct to grab for his gun, but the Arracks had disarmed him.

"I don't care what you want to call yourself, I know you as Marcus." Hank jumped to his feet, but Zach matched his movement in a flash, drawing his square gun. He shot an electrical charge, hitting Hank in the chest. Every muscle fired at the same time, sending him to the floor. His jaw clenched and his feet curled up as he convulsed.

The shock stopped and he breathed hard. His muscles released their intense grip and he felt control of his body returning. Two cords ran from his chest to the gun in Zach's hand. Hank tried to move, but his arms wouldn't work right. He lay on his side and watched Zach get close to Harris.

"I thought it would have been harder to capture *the* Harris." Zach hovered over him with his hand in his pocket. Harris's bloody hand grabbed Zach's throat, but Zach injected something into his neck. Harris's hand fell and he slumped over. "Don't worry, I've got enough for you too, Hank. You are part of the plan as well."

Hank felt the needle dip into his neck and soon, it was all black.

CHAPTER 22

JOEY LOOKED ON AS JULIE punched the off button on her cell phone. Hank hadn't been answering her phone calls and she seemed like she might throw her phone out the car window. "It could be a hundred reasons," he said, attempting to calm her. "Maybe the power's out, or maybe Harris told him to leave it behind."

Julie sighed. "Can we pull over? I have to . . . you know."

"Is this a number one or a number two pull over?" Lucas asked, glancing from her to the road as he drove.

Julie punched him. "I have to change a tampon, if you must know."

Lucas quickly veered off the road. The car bounced onto the bumpy shoulder as it came skidding to a stop.

Julie glared at him before opening the door. Dust swirled into the car. "Poly, can you come with me?"

"You need my help?"

"I don't want to be outside, in the dark, stuck with my pants around my ankles, in a post-apocalyptic America."

"Well, when you put it that way." Poly opened her door and they walked into the darkness off the highway.

Joey got out of the car as well and watched a car drive by, giving his back to the girls. A good Samaritan might have stopped, but he was glad they didn't. He didn't feel like talking to someone about the cure or how great it was. He'd heard enough on the radio. The whole world seemed to be celebrating the cure, but at what cost? He kicked the gravel along the shoulder of the exit. Even if they knew the costs, they'd still pay it.

Lucas walked around to the side of the car and leaned against it. "Seems like we don't get a moment, just the two of us, anymore."

Joey chuckled, but when he thought about it, he couldn't recall the last it was just him and Lucas. "Yeah, it's been a while."

Lucas moved closer and looked down at his arm. "How's it going, you know, with the shakes?"

"It comes and goes, but I feel pretty good. Poly helps."

"Yeah, she doesn't leave your side. She'd kill me if I brought up your condition."

"My condition?" Joey crossed his arms.

"Dude, you know how hard it is to not bust your balls over it?"

"So you've been holding back to save my feelings?" Joey asked.

Lucas looked confused. "No, I just don't want to get stabbed by Poly, dude. She freaking adores you."

"Yeah, she does . . . And, you know, Julie tolerates you. Which says a lot."

Lucas laughed. "That she does." He stared into the darkness. "You know, even with everything that has happened, I feel like we are two lucky guys to have people like Poly and Julie with us."

Joey turned to face Lucas. It wasn't very often the man went to a deeper emotional level. "I agree, bud. We are damned lucky."

"Hey, you think we are doing the right thing here? Maybe we could find a place to escape, a place Marcus would never think of looking," Lucas said.

"Like Nebraska?"

Lucas laughed. "No, there are other worlds, I think the Arracks know of them. Aren't you getting sick of this revolving door? Don't you want to wash your hands of it at some point?"

Joey wanted nothing more than to take Poly away from it all. He sighed. "I'm not leaving until we have Samantha. After that, we can talk."

Poly and Julie emerged from the darkness and walked up the shoulder toward the car.

"I hope I never have to outdoor pee again," Julie said.

Poly laughed. "You boys do okay without us?"

"Joey started getting all emo on me but yeah, we managed."

Poly turned her attention to Joey and raised an eyebrow. "You never get all emo with me."

"Well, Lucas wouldn't stop making fun of my shakes." Poly glared at Lucas. "He kept singing, Joey's milkshake brings all the girls to the yard and then he made me hold a box of chocolate milk."

She brandished her knife.

"He was right," Joey said putting a hand on Poly. "You *are* stopping him from making fun of me."

Poly glanced at him while Lucas hid behind an annoyed Julie. "Yeah, it's not something I want him joking about." She tried to move toward Lucas.

"Don't do that." He pulled her closer. "It's part of who I am now, and if we start acting different about it, it just makes it worse. I expect Lucas to take jabs at me, when he doesn't, it gets weird."

Poly took in a slow breath and sheathed her knife. "He didn't say any of those things, did he?" He shook his head. "Well, maybe I'm not ready to joke about it, okay? I mean you almost freaking killed yourself saving us. That shake is a reminder of the day I thought I lost you."

Joey sighed. "Maybe, but it still could be funny. If we can't laugh, we are not going to make it. I don't think the road ahead is going to get any easier. In fact, if Marcus has it in for us, it's only going to get a lot worse."

Poly studied Joey for a few seconds and then turned to Lucas. "Fine, but if you push the line, and I will judge what the line is . . . I will cut you."

"Okay," Lucas agreed. "Joey and I can shake hands on it." He stood and shook his hand at his side.

Joey laughed. That is what he really wanted. Having a physical problem didn't make you a different person, and he didn't want to be treated any differently. "I would shake hands with you, but is pale contagious? I don't want to look like Powder."

"Oh, this is a competition now?" Lucas said and tapped his finger on his chin. "How about a game of Jenga to settle this?"

Joey laughed.

"Have you guys got it out of your system yet?" Poly asked with her arms crossed.

"Oh come on. Joey's like my brother," Lucas said.

"Can we just get back to what we're going to do about Samantha? Anything is better than this."

Joey felt the smile leaving his face and the weight of the mission settling back on his shoulders.

"Joey's right about what might be ahead. I have a bad feeling about it," Julie said. "Samantha already went with this Zach guy once."

"She was injured and needed medical attention. She thought she was saving the world," Joey pointed out.

Poly frowned and took a deep breath as she looked at him. "All we can do is try."

"And if trying doesn't work, we'll stuff her in a box and take her away," Lucas added. "After, we can de-program her or something."

"Well, nothing is going to happen if we don't get there." Julie opened the car door and got in. "We should be there by morning, if traffic isn't too bad."

CHAPTER 23

SAMANTHA STIRRED AWAKE. HER HEAD pounded and she felt the thin carpet on her face and hands. Bright lights blinded her and for a brief moment, she thought she might have died and been shipped to heaven.

A silhouette of a man hovered over her, caressing her face.

"Joey?" She blinked, clearing her eyes. "Zach!" she exclaimed. In the thrill of seeing him, safe and at her side, she tried to lift herself up on one elbow. Closing her eyes, she palmed the side of her head, trying to find relief from her severe headache.

Zach knelt next to her and grabbed the back of her head, drawing her into his chest. She welcomed his embrace and wanted to get lost in his strong arms. "I'm sorry for the knockout gas. It was something of a safety protocol, part of thirty-two, and well . . . it was meant for intruders."

"Where are we?" Lisa asked, stirring from her spot on the ground. Her voice sounded different, as if it had a slight accent. Samantha had heard that accent somewhere.

"You are right where you fell," Zach explained.

Derek tried to move to his feet but only got as far as one knee. He lifted his hand to his head and swayed.

Samantha snuggled into Zach's chest. She thought he might've been killed or captured, but he wasn't; he was safe and with her. She wanted to grab him by the hand and pull him away from it all. They could escape to his house, to his bedroom. "Wait a minute." Her anger flared. She got to her feet and stabbed a finger at the screen showing his bedroom.

He gazed at the screen without emotion, studying it, as if trying to see what the issue was. Then he nodded his head, solving the problem. He turned to face her with a cool smile and took her by each arm. "No one is here at night, and we don't record from these monitors."

Lisa moved next to Zach, staring at his face. "You look different."

"As opposed to what? Have we met?"

Lisa blinked and took a step back, covering her mouth. "I . . . I just meant," she put her thumb and finger on her temples, "I just didn't expect you to look the way you look is all."

Zach smirked. "I hope it's a pleasant surprise."

"Oh yes. I mean, you're very good looking and all." Lisa stopped her words with thinned lips and promptly studied the floor, covering her forehead with her hand.

Samantha frowned at Lisa but turned her attention to Zach. "I want these cameras turned off if you ever think I'm going back to your place." She almost choked on her bold words. Even Lisa looked up from her floor inspection to witness the deluge of information.

"How about I shut them off right now?"

"Yes, please."

He typed into the computer and the camera switched to the parking lot of ZRB headquarters. "Better?"

"Much, thank you. And," she leaned in closer, "I want you to make sure there wasn't a recording."

His lips brushed her ear causing chills to run down her neck. She wanted more of him. "You sure? We might look great together on screen."

She flushed and pushed at his chest, smiling.

"Sir," Derek said. "We should secure the building in case we get attacked again."

"No need. The US government and I have come to an agreement," he said as if he had big news. "I want to give floor sixteen a party. We need to celebrate what we have accomplished. You are of course invited, Lisa."

"Yes, well, thank you," she said. "I already had pizza coming actually." She looked at her watch. "It should be here soon."

"You look familiar." Zach cocked his head. "Are you sure we haven't met? I usually don't forget a face, especially an employee."

"Not that I'm aware of."

"Well, let's make it official then," he said, putting out his hand. "I'm Zach Ryan Baker."

"Hello." She shook his hand. "I'm Lisa Gem."

"Gem? What an unusual last name. Italian?"

Lisa stammered, looking around the room. "I don't know. It's just a family name."

"Well, you are as beautiful as any gem I've seen."

"Thank you."

Samantha breathed hard through her nose and felt old feelings surfacing, feelings she never wanted again. Just the fact she felt them made her angrier, fueling her fire. She blazed at Lisa who looked as if she wanted to be anywhere in the world but where she was. At that moment Samantha didn't see the cute little Lisa, she saw Poly or another version of her, trying to get between her and her man.

Lisa glanced at her and then looked away.

Samantha grasped Zach's hand in hers and walked as best she could out of the monitoring room, trying to get Lisa from her mind. She couldn't have her parading around the office, flaunting her body like a little slut. Lisa would have to be fired right away.

She looked to Zach. "Can we discuss a few things?"

"Later, okay?" He stopped and took out his tablet. He scanned the screen and Samantha looked over his shoulder to take a peek, but he flipped pages too fast for her to make any sense of it. A jumble of pictures, she thought she made out a car in one of the pictures, and then a group of texts.

She saw the strain on his face. "Is there a problem?"

Zach sighed and looked back at Lisa.

If he looked at Lisa one more time, she was going to slap him.

"We have visitors. Friends of yours, from Preston."

CHAPTER 24

JOEY HAD EXPECTED THERE TO be some sort of security on ZRB's property, but nothing had impeded their progress. Poly pulled their car into the front lot and they all looked at the entrance to headquarters. Samantha's last phone signal came from behind those doors and they had every intention of getting her out.

"Well, this is it." Joey opened the door and they each got out of the car.

They crossed the parking and as they got closer, Joey saw the barricaded windows and doors on every floor. Julie said they were on some kind of lockdown, but it looked more like a prison. How were the people inside handling this lockdown? Could anyone leave? Judging by the parking lot full of cars, he guessed not.

"I think I can get the front door open," Julie said, face deep in her Panavice.

"No need, it's opening." Lucas pointed to the door.

Joey stopped. He spotted the door opening as well and watched as four people exited the building. Samantha's long, wavy hair flowed over her shoulders and Joey kept his attention on her as she walked a few steps behind Zach.

"Holy crap, there's Gladius," Lucas said.

Poly perked up and kept her eyes on Gladius. "Not a word, remember what Travis said, she was infiltrating ZRB from the inside."

Zach smiled. Joey held his breath and watched the man's hands as he approached. He adjusted his neck tie and played with a large tie clip. Harris had warned them Marcus was unbeatable in a gun draw, but he wouldn't just lay down and take it. He'd kill this guy if he could. Joey's shaky hand touched his gun.

Zach stopped short, but Samantha ran up to Julie and gave her a hug. Then she moved to Lucas.

Joey searched her face for the wounds she carried on the tarmac, but they were gone. She looked as good as ever.

"What are you doing here?" she asked.

"We came to get you," Lucas said.

Samantha looked confused and took several steps back. "What do you mean? We are sending out the cure to the entire world right now. I can't just leave, I'm needed here."

Joey wanted to laugh and shove down her throat the results of Travis's test, but he knew she wouldn't believe them. It was as if this Zach guy put a spell on her, and all rational thought left her brain.

"She's right, she's an invaluable part of the company and at this time, we simply couldn't afford to be without her," Zach said with his stupid perfect smile.

The smug look on his face as Samantha nodded in agreement drove Joey to the red zone. His shaky hand touched his gun again, and he saw Zach eyeing him. Probably waiting to get a jump on him. Joey knew he could never get past the man's shield.

"We can show you a few things to convince you," Joey said.

"What? Are you going to show me how he isn't saving the world? How he hasn't saved Preston and from what I hear, our families? Why can't you all leave this alone?"

"We just want you to come home, Samantha," Joey said and took a step closer. He wanted to take her hands and pull her away from Zach, just being close to them was nauseating.

"I *am* home. Don't you get it? I left Preston for a reason. I am trying to put this . . . *you*, past me. I don't want to go with you, I want to stay here."

"Samantha—"

"I know what this is. You're jealous of me." Samantha sniffled.

"Jealous of what?" Poly said.

"You don't get to talk!" She screamed, breathing hard. "I had to sit and watch you take Joey from me. I had to sit across the cafeteria and watch Hank, Lucas, and Julie go over to your side." She shook with emotion. "You all left me alone! And now I have a new home, new friends, and I am the one saving the world. I am the one making the difference, and it's killing you."

The anger in Joey slumped into a terrible mixture of guilt and regret. Julie had warned him he was going to break up the Six if he chose between Samantha and Poly. But he couldn't live without Poly by his side. His hatred for Marcus grew in size, thinking of how he'd created this wedge between them.

"Samantha, the only reason we are here is because we love you," Julie said. "We don't want to see this man, whoever he is, use you for his purposes. Think about it, who is he really? Does he have any background at all?"

Samantha glanced at Zach, who kept a slightly amused expression on his face, as if to say you can't be taking any of this seriously. She walked closer to Joey, within a foot. An armed guard moved closer, but Zach waved him off.

Joey took in a breath and held his ground.

She jabbed her finger in his chest and then pointed it at Julie and Lucas. "You all say you love me? Really? Does love make you abandon another friend because it's uncomfortable to be around her?" She stared down Julie and Lucas.

Joey opened his mouth but closed it. He looked at Julie and she shook her head as she skimmed the surface of her Panavice. She wasn't getting through his shield. Maybe they didn't need to. He pulled his gun and pointed it at Zach.

Zach raised his hands just above his face and wiggled them like jazz hands. A big smile spread across his face. "No, Derek, put it away. We are not shooting these people, no matter what."

Derek lowered his gun and holstered it. Joey kept his gun trained on Zach's head. "I'm going to prove to you right now, who this man truly is, Samantha."

She moved her body in front of Zach and sneered. "I won't let you kill him. This man saved the world."

"He's actually the one who started the whole epidemic," Julie said.

Samantha crossed her arms. "I know what kind of man he is and he's not the person you think he is. Does he even *look* like Marcus?"

"He must have changed his appearance or something, but all of his actions and advanced technology point to who he is," Julie explained.

Zach seemed highly amused by the conversation and kept his hands in the air.

Samantha scowled at Julie and then pointed at Joey. "Put that gun down, Joey Foust."

She looked as if she hated him, but the look pushed his resolve. Once she saw the bullet bounce off him, she'd know he wasn't from Earth. She'd be forced to acknowledge they were right. And maybe in time, she could forgive them.

Zach side stepped Samantha and exposed his body with a smile, still with his hands in the air. Samantha hadn't noticed and Joey pulled back on the trigger. The gun fired and Zach staggered backward, holding his shoulder. Blood trickled over his hand.

"Don't shoot them, Derek!" Zach screamed.

Derek already had his gun trained on Joey, but Joey only had eyes for the wound on Zach's shoulder. The man didn't have a shield. He must have turned it off.

"Zach!" Samantha rushed to his side. "What did you do, Joey?" she cried out. Her hands pushed against his shoulder and Zach winced in pain.

"I thought he would have a shield, like on the tarmac." Joey looked on, dumbfounded. "He's playing a game with us or something. This isn't right."

"You'll pay for this," Samantha spewed.

Joey staggered back.

"Help me, Derek." The guard grabbed Zach's arm and helped walk him toward the building.

Samantha turned and thundered toward them. Tears and rage filled her face. "Don't you *ever* come back to me again, any of you. Stay out of my life! You understand?"

They did and Joey couldn't find the words to make it better. He only watched as Samantha ran to Zach's side. Gladius glanced at them and back to Zach. She shrugged her shoulders and ran toward Samantha.

Since the first day they'd found the stone, he'd been physically hurt in every way possible, but this hurt worst of all.

"*That* didn't go well," Lucas said.

"You think?" Julie said.

"I thought you said he had his shield up?" Joey asked.

"I thought I had something," Julie said, fiddling with her Pana. "It was like he was transmitting and receiving a signal at all times, but I couldn't pin it down."

"She's all in now," Poly said. "We made it worse."

Joey turned and found Julie. "What did you find if not his shield? What is it?"

"I don't know. With a bit more time with him, I could find out, but he's connected to something or someone out there."

"Could he be connected to—" Poly started to say.

"I found something in that building," Julie said. Her face went pale and she looked at the building, eyes traveling to the upper floors.

"What?" Lucas asked.

"Renee."

"Oh great, that psycho computer is freaking in there." Lucas shook his head.

Julie's face went back to her Panavice. "I couldn't see her right away, but she is drawing massive power. . . ."

Poly could tell she was holding back something. "What's weird about it?"

"I don't know, it feels too obvious."

"Maybe to you, but would anyone else suspect anything?"

"No, but if we don't stop her, she could do much worse things than blowing up Panavices in a world like this. I mean, she could start launching nukes, or take out entire nuclear power plants. She is far more dangerous here than on Vanar. Our systems aren't set up to handle an attack from a super computer."

"Fine, I'll go in and kill her, just like her sister," Lucas said.

"Oh my God." Julie shook her head, looking even paler as she stared at her screen. "No."

"Great, what is it now?" Lucas asked.

"You remember when Max put trackers in our necks?" She said, looking at each of them in the eyes.

"Yes, but you disabled them," Poly said.

"I did, but when we got back home I sort of played with their codes, finding a way to hide a signal in them among all the digital noise. No one would ever find them if they didn't have my program."

"What does this all mean?" Joey asked, growing impatient.

"It means I'm picking up a signal in that building and it's not Samantha..." She shoved her screen in Joey's face, pointing at the blinking red dot. "It's Hank."

CHAPTER 25

"WE SHOULD HAVE KILLED THEM," Derek said as he paced next to Zach laying on the lobby floor.

"Get me a medical bag!" Samantha demanded, kneeling next to Zach. She removed Zach's shirt as carefully as she could. When he winced, she winced. She thought maybe Zach would get shot at some point—creating something everybody needed to stay alive meant you had the whole world wanting to take it from you—but she never imagined the bullet would come from Joey Foust.

Anger filled her again thinking about it. He'd done it to prove a point and all he accomplished was proving how wrong he was. She almost agreed with Derek in that moment, like she wouldn't know if Zach was the vilest person ever . . . Did they really think she was so stupid?

Blood was smeared over a healthy portion of his body. Samantha held her hand over her mouth, but she recovered from the shock and pulled open the bag Derek set next to her.

Lisa stood nearby. She hadn't said a word since the shooting.

"Can you help me with this?" Samantha asked.

Lisa looked pale and took a few steps back. "I can't, I just can't." She turned and ran out of the lobby.

"I've had some training." Derek dropped on his knees next to her.

Samantha took a step back and felt tears flowing down her face. How could her friends have done this? She didn't even know if she could learn to forgive them.

"I'm going to be fine," Zach said with a smile. He seemed amused by the whole gunshot thing.

"I'm not sure, Zach," Derek said putting pressure over his wound. The gauze turned red. "You're losing a lot of blood. We need to get you to a hospital."

"Thanks, but all I need you to do is take me to my medical wing on floor thirteen."

"We don't have a facility to operate on you."

"Listen," Zach sat up and the fire in his eyes made Derek lean back. "Take me to floor thirteen, now."

"Let's just take him there," Samantha interjected.

Derek nodded and grabbed Zach's arm, lifting him on his feet. Samantha rushed to his side and supported him. They walked Zach to the stairs.

After thirteen flights, Samantha thought she was the one needing a medical team. She held on to Zach, breathing hard.

"The back room." Zach pointed. They helped him walk to the door. "Now leave me." He shrugged off their help and leaned against the door with one hand.

"Sir, you are in—"

"I said, leave me," he barked.

Derek took a few steps back, turned and walked out of the room.

"I can help you." Samantha rubbed his bare shoulder, feeling his sweat cover her hand.

"Please, just go. I will be fine in a bit. I have a doctor in here who will help me."

Samantha stared at the solid steel door and wondered why she never heard they had a doctor on staff, let alone a medical room advanced enough to handle a gunshot wound. But she didn't know about the whole surveillance floor either. She started thinking about all the things she didn't know and they were mounting quickly.

"I'll be waiting out here."

"Fine, but please wait in the stairwell."

"Okay." She bumped into a monitor displaying what looked like a burnt forest, but she didn't give it much thought as she stared at Zach's bare back. Turning quickly, she left the room, watching him from the stairwell. He stood at the door and she heard his voice and a faint vibrating sound before the door opened. He entered the door and it closed behind him.

SAMANTHA SAT ON THE FLOOR of the stairwell. Her butt hurt and she adjusted herself, trying to find a more comfortable spot. Zach had been in the room for a while, she'd even knocked on the door a few times, but no one answered. Thoughts of him lying dead on the floor filled her mind. She couldn't help it. She kept thinking of the worst possible scenarios. She got up, unable to sit, and paced, staring at the steel door.

The door opened and she ran toward it.

Derek ran on her heels and Zach exited the room, wearing a clean black shirt with his tie clip pinned to it. He looked weary, but the color was back in his face. She tried to sneak a look in the room as the door closed, but she only saw a glass machine that looked like a tanning bed.

He smiled and held out his hands. "All better."

She rushed to him and hugged him, kissing his mouth. She didn't want to ever let him leave her sight again. It was just her and him from now on. If she was braver, she would have said the three words to him right then and there.

"Not totally better," he said between her kisses.

"Glad to see you're okay, sir," Derek said.

Zach ignored him and used his hands to caress Samantha's face. She felt him kissing her back. His tongue brushed her lips and she moaned. She pushed her body against his, and clutched on to him.

He breathed heavy and pushed her back to look at Derek. "Can you get my helicopter ready?"

"Yes, sir," Derek said and jogged to the staircase.

With Derek gone, Zach turned his attention to Samantha. She loved the lust in his eyes, she felt the same way.

"Let's wait until we get back to the house," Zach suggested.

"You sure you're okay?"

"I'm fine." He looked back at the door. "I have a great doctor."

"Can I thank him for fixing my man?" She brushed her fingers down his back and pulled his hips against her own.

"Wouldn't you rather get out of here?" Zach said.

Yes, more than anything, she wanted to be somewhere alone with Zach. She would follow him to where ever he wanted to go. Kissing him again, she took as much from him as she could.

"A friend told me recently that a tragic situation can bring a couple together, closer than ever. I didn't understand it until now."

"I don't know if I can get any closer," Samantha said, pushing up against him.

"Transport's ready, sir," Derek announced, standing at the doorway.

"Great, can you take Samantha up there? I have one item I need to attend to before I can join you both."

"Yes, of course."

"But. . . ." Samantha pouted.

"Just a moment longer, my dear. I'll be up there before you can miss me too much."

"Not possible. I miss you and you're standing in front of me."

"Let your need grow, and when we are together it will be all the greater."

Samantha didn't want to let go, but Zach moved away from her and took her hand, guiding her to Derek.

Derek pulled on her arm, climbing the stairs with her. She looked back at Zach standing on the landing, looking up at her. They rounded the next steps and he was gone. She reluctantly followed Derek to the roof, where Zach's helicopter sat in wait, motors roaring and blades spinning.

ZACH STOPPED WAVING AND TOOK off his stupid smile. He tasted his lips, still wet from her tongue. It wasn't a bad flavor, but he couldn't let the thoughts of tasting her distract him from his goal. He had a lady to find.

He ran down the stairs, knowing exactly where to find her; the floor with the cure. The steps flew by as he skipped down four at a time. The door hung open to the research wing where he supposedly found the cure. Now, where was she?

"Hello?" Zach called out.

"Don't move." Lisa pointed a shotgun at his head from across the room.

Too far to snatch from her delicate hands, Zach laughed at the aggression. He didn't expect her to be so easy to find. He could dispatch her in a few minutes and be back to Samantha in no time. "Dear, *Lisa*. It looks like you won't be playing the charade anymore?"

"Who are you? You are not Marcus." She gripped the gun with both hands.

He took a step closer and raised his hands. "I am your savior."

Lisa lowered her hand and pulled a Panavice from her pocket. "I've seen what's in your serum. I don't know what you are planning on doing, but I won't let you do it. These people are good. They've shown me more respect and kindness than all of Vanar."

Zach took a step closer and lowered his hands slightly. "I have a feeling you don't know how to use that weapon. Did daddy not teach you? Or was it your mother who never allowed you to touch something so crude?"

Lisa shook. "Shut your mouth. It ends now. It ends here." Lisa pulled the trigger, sending a shower of sparks out of the barrel.

He didn't move as the pellets bounced off his shield.

She fired again, but with the same results. Zach laughed and took several steps closer. Bits of paper floated around and the smell of gunsmoke filled the room.

Lisa dropped the gun and picked up a long dagger from the table. It melded with her movements as if an extension of her body.

"There you go, that's your weapon. Look at you."

"Just come for it, you sick bastard."

"Oh, I will, but that doesn't mean we can't have fun. Do you want to have fun with me?"

She rushed toward him and slammed her dagger against his shield. He reached out in a flash, grabbing her wrist and squeezing it near the breaking point.

"This is what I'm talking about." Zach pulled her closer and nuzzled against her neck. "You're a pretty thing, aren't you?"

She struggled and it made him laugh, holding her even tighter, he wouldn't let her go until he got what he wanted. Then he felt it, a stabbing pain at his side. He looked down and saw a wooden dagger piercing his shirt and penetrating his skin.

He laughed again and she pushed it further. He felt the warm blood filling his innards.

"Just die!"

"Not now, not ever." He pulled her hand back, snapping the small bones in her arm. She cried out in pain. He head butted the side of her head and let her fall to the ground.

A wooden knife? What a cunning little bitch. He kicked her in the stomach and raised his foot over her unconscious head, but stopped. *No.* He had a plan to follow. A path to travel. He grabbed her by her wrist and dragged her limp body down the stairs.

At the bottom, he placed his hand on the wall and activated the screen. Typing in the code, he said the password. "I am the savior."

The floor slid open, revealing another set of stairs. He felt like pushing her body down the final set of stairs, but he didn't want to damage her beyond repair. He could have fun with such a body for a long time.

He dragged her down the four flights of stairs to another sealed door. He used a retinal scan to open the final door. A simple warehouse, really. Blank walls and a high ceiling for which to hang a person from. He admired simple things.

"Let us down from here," Hank called out.

Zach slid Lisa's body across the floor, under Hank and Harris. They both looked down at his new prize. Zach took out his tablet and used it to lower the chain from the ceiling. He tied up Lisa's arms and raised the chain until she was dangling unconscious. "I brought you company." He walked up to Harris and patted his dangling foot. He tried to kick Zach, but he ducked under it. He looked up to Harris. "You can talk, but don't touch . . . her body's mine."

Harris eyed him and the simple act unnerved Zach. The man seemed to be taking in everything he did, judging it.

Shaking it off, he reminded himself it didn't matter anymore. Soon, the plan would be complete and he could be free. Being so close to the end sent chills up his arms and he ignored the calls from Hank.

"Don't worry, I'll be back soon and we can finish this. Hang in there." He laughed his way out of the room, grabbing at his side. He needed to get to floor thirteen before meeting Samantha on the roof.

She really was gorgeous, and he felt a hint of shame at what he was doing to her, but squashed it quickly. The plan required him to do certain things, in the correct order, if he wanted to ever be free. She was just a means to an end.

CHAPTER 26

HANK SWAYED FROM THE CHAIN, the leather straps digging into his wrists. He made sure not to say anything until the door closed and Zach was gone. "Gladius," he whispered.

Harris stared at her swaying between them.

At first she didn't move, but then a smile crept in and she opened her eyes, gazing at the closed door. "Hey, Hank. Hey, Harris."

"How the hell did he get to you?" Hank asked.

"I was pretending to be a new employee at ZRB and got all the way up to Samantha's assistant." Gladius struggled against her straps and rattled the chain running up into the ceiling. "If I had to be that freaking, bubbly Lisa girl for one more minute..."

"You sneaky little—wait, did he hit you?" Hank asked.

"That dude head-butted me freaking hard." She adjusted her hands and the chain clanked under her movement. "Did it leave a mark?" She looked to the side, revealing a large swath of red and swollen skin along the side of her face.

Hank gritted his teeth and looked at the floor.

She growled. "I knew it. I'm going to cut his balls off if my face guy can't fix this. At least he took me down here."

"You *wanted* down here?"

"Well, yeah. Who else was going to save your stupid asses?" She did a double take at

Harris. "If my face looks anything like yours, I'll slit my wrists and end it all."

Harris laughed and then coughed. "You have a plan?"

"Of course."

Hank wanted to hug Gladius. She was one of the last people in the worlds he expected to see coming to their rescue.

She glanced at him and smiled. "What? Did you think I was going to let you guys deal with this by yourself?"

"I didn't think you . . . No, not really. I am thrilled to see you, though," Hank said. He recalled the few times they went to Vanar over the last year, making appearances for her dad. She was always around and they had pleasant conversations, but he never felt he made any kind of lasting impression.

"Can you tell us this plan?" Harris said and then coughed. "You have a light saber bracelet or are you just going to use the force?"

"A *Stars Wars* reference, nice, Harris. You watched the box set Lucas gave you, didn't you?"

He laughed. "Yes, some fine movies."

"If you nerds are done nerding, can we go now?" Gladius now hung by one arm. She dropped from the chain and landed on her feet. Looking up, she walked to the wall and pressed a button. Hank heard motors running as they were lowered to the ground. She pulled Harris free and he slumped to the ground.

"Get Hank free, don't worry about me."

She complied and went to Hank. He felt her petite hands untying the straps and freeing his hands. Once they were released, he wrapped her up in a hug and spun her in a circle.

"I didn't know I was going to get a ride for my deed." She patted Hank on the shoulders and giggled.

"I would give you so much more if I had it."

Harris fell forward onto his hands and coughed blood on the floor. He recovered and looked up at them. "To tell you the truth, I was positive I was going to die on the chains up there. Until the moment I saw that man dragging you into this room. I knew then I had a chance."

"Aren't you sweet? Thinking my limp body was going to be your saving grace."

"It wasn't you, it was him. The last time I saw him, I was nearly unconscious and took his imitation for face value. His walk, his voice, his mannerisms were nearly dead on, but today he made a critical mistake."

"What, being an extra-large asshole?" Gladius asked.

"No, his laugh. I've heard it only a few times in my life and Marcus doesn't laugh like that."

"Wait, are you saying this Zach guy isn't Marcus?" Hank asked.

Gladius snorted. "Duh, just look at him."

"I thought he changed his looks or something. I mean, my friends were pretty convinced he was the guy." Hank let it all soak in and asked the question they all had. "If he isn't Marcus, who is he?"

"More importantly, what is he doing?" Harris said.

"He has to be, who else could control the Arracks like this?" Hank said. "Why play with us this way? Why not just kill us? I mean, he knows who we are, he knows where you came from."

"He knew who I was as well. I saw it on his face the second he looked at me," Gladius added.

Harris shook his head and gingerly got to his feet. "He could be faking he is faking. A long time ago, before Marcus became the evil man you know him as, he was a fun loving guy. He would play pranks, and just mess with people around him for the fun of it. We used to call him a joker."

"Marcus?" Hank and Gladius spoke at the same time.

"I think he used it early on to cope with his intelligence. He wanted to interact with people and found it difficult to relate to most. But there was venom behind the smile, once you got to know him."

"Then why this charade?"

"If it is Marcus using the façade of Zach, then we are in greater danger than I imagined.

He must be planning something grand and I bet it all centers around us, and the rest of the group. Have you seen him interacting with any of the Six?"

"Are you kidding? His girlfriend is Samantha, and she hangs all over his nuts like a squirrel getting ready for winter. Makes me ill." Gladius rolled her eyes.

"Samantha?" Hank asked.

"Yeah, they are like boyfriend-girlfriend." She made a rude gesture with her fingers.

"Marcus rarely takes on a girlfriend; if he does, it's only for another reason."

"So now we are thinking this Zach guy *is* Marcus?" Hank asked.

"It doesn't matter. Whoever he is, we need to stop him and warn the rest. Marcus is the type of person who will go to great lengths and spend a lot of time driving his point home to an opponent."

"That should be easy, as the rest of the six are right outside," Gladius said. "We just had an encounter with them. Joey freaking shot Zach. It was awesome." She laughed.

"The rest are *here*?" Harris asked.

"Yeah, they should still be out there."

"We need to get to them."

"No offense, but you look terrible. Can you even walk?" Gladius said.

Harris took a step and closed his swollen eyes, before making his way toward the door. Favoring one leg, he stopped and stabbed his finger at the screen on the wall in frustration. After a minute of messing with the screen, he took a step back. "I can't get through it."

"I bet Julie can get down here." Gladius pulled out what looked like a dice.

"You brought a ping?" Harris said and moved closer.

"Yes, if you know her Panavice ID, we can send her a text."

"I do know it." Harris took the dice in his hand and pressed his finger on it. It unfolded into a screen the size of a playing card.

Hank shook his head as he looked on. He was always amazed by the technology they used.

"Tell her about the door under the stairs. Tell her the password above is 'I am the savior,'" Gladius said.

"What an arrogant. . . ." Harris mumbled the rest under his breath as he typed into the screen. "Okay, sent it. Maybe she will have better luck getting through this door."

"Let's hope she does it quickly. I have a feeling that dirt bag will be back soon. I bet he finishes up with Samantha in a hurry."

JOEY WATCHED JULIE GLARE AT her screen with unblinking eyes. They'd formed a small circle around her at the bottom of the stairs inside the ZRB headquarters.

"Holy crap, Harris and Gladius are down there with him too. They gave me the password to the door." Julie had gotten past all the other security protocols, but the password on the floor door had blocked her.

"Let's bust this door down then," Lucas said.

Julie slid her hand across the screen on the floor and said, "I am your savior." The door opened, revealing a staircase.

Joey rushed down, wanting to get to Hank and Harris. Another steel door stood in their way.

Julie walked up and smiled. "This one's easy."

Soon, the door slid open and Hank rushed out. The big guy looked weary and his wrists were raw and red. Joey paused for a second when he saw Harris. The man looked like he'd been severely beaten with much of his face black from bruising; not to mention the swelling, which made him almost unrecognizable.

"Hank!" Lucas yelled and jumped into his arms.

"So good to see you guys." Hank took turns hugging everyone.

It felt good to have the big guy back in the mix. It lessened the sting from Samantha a smidgen, but it still weighed on Joey's mind more than anything else. He didn't see a way to convince her anymore.

"Are those tears?" Lucas pointed to Hank's face. "Are you *crying*?"

"No, there is just a lot of dust down here," Hank said, wiping his eyes.

"Dude, there is no dust down here." Lucas laughed. He wrapped his arms around him in a man hug and then moved to Harris. "Dear God, what the hell happened to you? Did you walk down a flight of stairs with your face?"

"Gladius," Julie squealed and ran up to her. They hugged and Joey thought he saw Gladius tearing up as well. "Why in the world are you here?"

She looked at the floor and stuffed her hands in her pocket. "I just thought I could help you guys."

"Ah, you are the sweetest thing," Poly said. "Thank you so much for coming to help us."

"Should we be talking in here?" Gladius asked, touching her face.

"I've scanned it. It's clear. Who did that to your face?" Julie asked.

Gladius brushed back a strand of her hair, revealing a red mark. "That bastard, Zach. But I found the serum he made, he put something in it."

"We know, your dad helped us find the nanobot," Julie said.

"I bet he's going to hold the whole world hostage with it," Lucas said. "I'm so glad we took the clean cure from Vanar." He stared at Harris again. "Dude, for real, what the hell happened to you? You look about as bad as Hank does on a good day."

Harris's swollen mouth crept back in a grin. "I was gang banged by a bunch of Arracks."

Lucas's mouth hung open for a second. "Wait, what does that mean on Vanar?"

"When a gang beats the crap out of you."

Lucas sighed in relief. "My God, man. Don't use that phrase here ever again. It means something much worse."

Harris laughed and smirked. "Got you."

"You sly bastard, you are not allowed to make jokes. You had me going for a second there."

"But really, a bunch of Arracks beat the crap out of me," Harris said.

"Yeah, they lined up like kids at an amusement park to get their hits in," Hank explained.

"It's for what you did to them, isn't? For attempting genocide and killing their planet?" Julie asked.

"Yes."

"Then you deserved it," she shot the words at Harris.

"I do and so much more."

Joey stepped between the two. "We need to work together if we have any chance of stopping Marcus. He has Samantha wrapped up in some kind of brainwashing."

"Love," Gladius corrected.

Joey felt like she punched him. Love? The word didn't fit. It had to mean something different on Vanar. "You're wrong, she doesn't love him. He must be slipping her drugs." He grasped for any logical reason to explain the path she'd taken. Poly squirmed by his side.

Gladius chuckled and shook her head. "I know what it looks like. The way you look at Poly." She pointed at Poly. "Samantha looks at Zach like that, but maybe with even more passion. I'm pretty sure they are back at his house right now. Your little show outside gave her every reason to fall completely on board with the scumbag."

He wouldn't let the thought sink in. Slamming his eyes shut, Joey thought of something he could control. "We are going to have to kill him."

"He's got his shield back up, I tried to kill him," Gladius said. "Not before I stuck him with my wooden knife. My dad told me their shield might not block slow moving wood."

"Good, there is a way to get past it then." Joey felt some relief. "We just need to get to his house and stop him once and for all."

"Don't you get it?" Julie said. "We've been one step behind this whole time. Or even worse, we're doing exactly what he wants while he laughs. I'm done following his crumb trail."

"Here, here," Lucas wrapped her up in a hug, but she pushed him away.

"Couldn't have said it better myself," Harris said. "We can't continue to chase anymore. I say we do something he won't be expecting."

"What, give up?" Gladius asked and rolled her eyes.

"Yes," Poly said. Some of them protested but she shushed them. "We don't give up on stopping Zach, but we give up on Samantha. He is expecting us to try and get her back at all costs, but I say we use her love for Zach against them. It would definitely be unexpected."

"And let's not forget about his digital freak of a mother." Lucas crossed his arms and looked up. Somewhere above them rested Renee.

"Yes, I've been thinking on that since the moment she contacted us," Julie said.

"Well, this plan might take care of both problems," Poly said as she laid out a plan.

They laid out their plan, and while Joey didn't like the danger it put Samantha in, he agreed, it was their best shot at ending it all. It involved making a trip to Vanar and splitting up the five people he cared for deeply. But if it worked, they'd have their planet back and hopefully, in time, they'd get Samantha to understand what they had to do.

CHAPTER 27

SAMANTHA COULDN'T KEEP HER MOUTH off Zach for the whole ride to his house. She explored his body with unabashed excitement as he returned her affections with fervor.

Their first time had seemed rushed; almost reserved and uncomfortable. But that was then. Now, she threw away her inhibitions and let her man carry her from the helicopter pad with her legs wrapped tightly around his body.

Zach pushed their bedroom door open and slammed her against the bed. He took off his tie clip and slid it on the lamp shade, then had his shirt off in a second. She reeled from seeing only a red spot from where the bullet had hit his shoulder. Another red line crossed his stomach and she meant to ask him about it, but he crawled on the bed, hungry for her. She sat up and inspected his wound, even ran her finger over its smooth remnants.

He took her hand in his, noticing her curious expression. "I have the best doctor in the world."

"I guess so. It's truly amazing. I haven't seen this kind of healing since. . . ." She trailed off. The man wouldn't have a clue where or what Vanar was. How was she ever going to explain her past to him? She didn't want to keep any secrets. She could tell him tomorrow or the next day.

Zach reached into his pocket and pulled out his cell phone. He slid his finger across the screen and the lights in the room went out. "Now you don't have to look at it."

"I don't mind, I like seeing you."

"You do," he smiled. "You know, in time, when we've saved the world, there will be a time for us."

"I know." Samantha's thoughts ran wild with having Zach to herself, no worldwide trips or endless meetings. "I love you." It slipped out and she covered her mouth.

He stopped moving and she wondered if she had said it too soon, maybe he didn't feel the same way. A feeling of inadequacy crashed over her.

Zach smiled and then whispered in her ear, "I've been waiting for you to say that."

It wasn't the response she wanted, but he started kissing her on the neck, shutting any thoughts from her mind.

SAMANTHA GLANCED BACK AT ZACH, getting his underwear back on. She resisted the urge to throw him on the bed and take him again. She wanted more.

Her phone dinged. She pulled it from her pants on the bathroom floor and looked at the blinking light. No one knew her number. It was a text message.

Unknown: This is Julie. I miss you so much, please just give me another chance. I only want you to be happy. I had no idea Joey was going to go all crazy like that. I think his slow-mo crap scrambled his brain.

Samantha grimaced at the message. She wanted to throw her phone in the toilet because she didn't want to be pulled back into her old life. She never wanted to think about anything else but her and Zach and their future together. She hated thinking of Joey as damaged from what he'd done. He'd saved them all from the Arrack world. He'd saved her from the scene generator. Those were facts she couldn't escape. As much as she wanted to hate him, she couldn't get all the way there.

Samantha: I miss you too, but I have a new life now. I don't want to deal with all the crap back home. Please, just leave me alone.

Unknown: I need something from you.

Samantha: ?

Unknown: We are going to the San Fran factory right now. Can you get us the entry code?

Samantha: Absolutely NOT. Are you serious? Haven't you done enough? Go away.

She pressed send and turned it off. Julie infuriated her. She couldn't believe she actually asked for codes to a factory. Like she would ever let them sabotage her company. She stared at her phone's blank screen, thinking of turning it back on and telling Julie off some more.

Oh God, she felt tears swelling in her eyes. She didn't like to have these mean thoughts about Julie. Sliding her thumb to the power button, a hand rubbed against her shoulder. She jumped and yelped. "Jesus, you scared me."

"I'm sorry, baby." He pulled at her loose shirt, bringing her body firmly against his. "Who are you texting?"

"Oh, just Julie, she was trying to convince me to come home again." She hated lying to him. The voice in her head screamed to tell him they were trying to break into a factory of theirs.

"She's a good friend?"

"She was, they all were. By the way, I'm so sorry Joey shot you. Man, that sounds terrible. I mean, he *shot* you."

"It's okay. They are trying to protect you. They think I'm this Marcus guy. He must be all kinds of bad for you guys to hate him so much."

"You have no idea." Samantha sighed. She wanted to tell him their history, but not just yet. "I'll make sure they never shoot you again."

He laughed. "Anytime you want to visit with them, let me know and we can get you a ride straight there—alone of course."

She wrapped her arms over his shoulders and moved close to his face. "I don't want to be anywhere but here, with you." She kissed him softly.

"You can stay, but we do have some business pending back at headquarters."

"Oh no, already?"

"Yeah."

"Can't it wait?" She looked at the bed and wanted more of him.

Looking amused, he grabbed her hands and held them. "I want you to come with me. I have something I want to show you."

"I'm invited on one of Zach Ryan Baker's trips?" She looked more shocked than she felt.

"Oh come on, we'll be spending plenty of time together. But I really want you to see something at headquarters. Something I've been planning on showing you for a long time."

Her interest peaked and her imagination ran wild. "If you put it like that, how can I say no? Let me get dressed."

"DON'T LET ME FALL." SAMANTHA hated surprises, but she kept the blindfold. She hadn't even known that headquarters had a basement.

"Last door's up here."

She reached the level surface of the floor and let him guide her. She instinctively held her hand out. Another door opened and a light breeze brushed past her. Zach dropped her arm and stomped away from her. "Zach?" She heard him in the distance, grunting in what she thought was frustration. "Everything okay?"

"Just take the damned blindfold off."

She pulled it free from her face, thinking she might see a car, a plane, maybe even a ring; *anything* but the large warehouse in front of her. Only a few chains dangled from the ceiling in an otherwise empty warehouse. She didn't get it and expressed her confusion to Zach.

"It's gone." He seemed mad, madder than she'd ever seen him.

"What's gone?"

He stormed past her and back to the staircase. "Where was Julie when she texted you?"

"I don't know. How did you even know she—"

Zach grabbed her arm and pulled her cell phone from her pocket.

"You're hurting me." She'd never seen this side of him and it was freaking her out. His face contorted with anger. Something very bad had happened.

He turned it on and scrolled through the screens. "The San Fran factory? Does this sound like 'I don't know' to you?" He pressed the phone toward her face.

"They just wanted the codes and you can see right there I told them no way."

"How did they even get this number? It's completely off grid. The only way is if you gave them the number." He threw the phone against the floor. It shattered into many pieces and clattered across the concrete floor.

"I didn't give them anything. She must have just hacked into the system. She's very good at that sort of thing."

"Really? Is she *very good*?" He mocked her. Pacing, he held his hand to his ear. "I know, I know."

"Why are you acting like this?" She started sobbing.

Zach didn't look up and kept pacing. "Fine." He lowered his hand from his ear and adjusted his tie clip.

"You're scaring me."

Zach closed his eyes, took a deep breath, and looked at the ceiling. "I'm sorry. I thought I'd have a large part of my plan for you completed, but now it's gone and I have to wait longer." Some of the sweet came back into his voice and his face was all smiles as he edged closer to her. The speed in which he switched emotions was startling.

She wiped her nose and stared at him with caution. "Just don't get all scary like that again, okay?"

"I'm so sorry. I just really wanted to give you this surprise, and someone must have stolen it from us."

"What was it?"

"And spoil the surprise? I think not. But don't worry, you'll find out soon enough. Now, why don't we take a trip to the factory, just to make sure your friends don't get into trouble?"

The thought of finding her friends there terrified her. What if they wanted to kill Zach again? Or maybe he'd hurt them? The idea of anybody getting hurt over her made her ill. "Why don't we just go back to the house? You can show me this present some other time."

"Oh no, this can't wait. Your friends may have stolen it and perhaps we can get it back."

"I don't want you hurting them."

"I won't touch them, you have my word."

She nodded her head and he smiled. Holding out his arm, he escorted her from the vacant warehouse. She glanced back. What present could he have possibly been storing under headquarters?

"HOW MUCH LONGER?" SAMANTHA ASKED, more anxious than she wanted to.

"We're here."

The helicopter landed in the parking lot. Zach didn't wait for her as he rushed out of it, running toward the factory. The front doors were only a few hundred feet from the copter and as she approached Zach from behind, she saw what he was staring at—a piece of paper taped to the door.

"It's for you," he said with his back facing her.

She pulled the paper free from the glass. *Six* was written on it. She turned it over but there was nothing on the back side. She recognized Julie's handwriting.

"It's a calling card. They didn't get into the building, and as far as I can tell, all they did was leave this note."

"Why?"

Zach rubbed his chin and turned to face her. Some of the dangerous look was back in his eyes. She used to think it was exciting, but when it was directed at her it was terrifying. "Your friends sent us here as a diversion." His eyes narrowed and he pushed past her.

"Where are we going?"

He didn't answer, so she rushed to catch up and got back into the helicopter. It took off before she could get her seatbelt on. Zach didn't wear a seatbelt and jerked around in his seat, mumbling to himself. He pulled out his tablet and looked up at her before tilting the screen so she couldn't see it.

He typed with his thumbs and she watched as he became more agitated. After a few minutes, he slammed the tablet on his lap and stuffed it back in his pocket.

"Everything okay?"

"No, take a look ahead." He pointed to the window.

She stared out at a distant glow. As they got closer she saw their destination was his house, but it was covered in flames. The inferno reached high above the house, twisting and turning into the sky. She stared at it, not believing it as real. It was obviously who'd done it. Why were they doing this to her?

The helicopter landed on the lawn. Even from the window, she saw a stake in the grass with a piece of paper flapping in the breeze. The *Six* could be seen from their location on the helicopter.

"They burned your house down," she whispered.

"They did more than that. I had an . . . important server in there." He cussed and slammed a fist into his seat.

"What ser—"

"Shit! Headquarters. . . ." He stood up and yelled directions at the pilot.

CHAPTER 28

POLY STOOD NEXT TO JOEY in the president's office. She missed all the blades once displayed and searched around the room for the few remnants of his old office. Joey nudged her and she focused on Travis standing in front of them.

"You two make a cute couple," Travis said, rounding his desk to sit on the edge.

"Thanks," Poly said. Travis spent far too much time staring at her. She shifted around under his gaze. She thought of the nights dancing with him and the kiss he stole in the apartment.

Joey cleared his throat. "Yeah, well, Mr. President—"

"Please call me Travis."

"Yes, okay. I'd like to thank you for taking Harris in. I think he was much worse than he was telling us."

Travis sucked in a deep breath. "Fortunately for him, there is little I won't do for you guys. Harris should be fine in few days."

Joey nodded and continued. "I know you didn't want to help us before, but we have all but confirmed this Zach guy as Marcus and we could use some help to stop him."

Poly huffed, like she needed another person with blades to help her. All they really needed was his stone.

"I will help, of course. But if this guy is Marcus, we won't have much of a chance."

"Gladius stabbed him with a wooden knife," Poly said.

He smiled and stood from his perch on the corner of his desk. "If she lived to tell the tale, then I doubt very much this man is Marcus."

"I hope he is. It needs to end with this," Poly said.

THE WIND PUSHED OUT TEARS from his eyes as Hank drove the motorcycle hard. He saw the headquarters in the distance and twisted the throttle, shifting into a higher gear. The roads were clear as he approached. In the last thousand feet, he turned the bike off and coasted. Steering the bike into the ravine behind the parking lot, he put out the kickstand.

Gladius was sprawled on her stomach a hundred feet ahead, facing the headquarters building. He ran over and laid down next to her.

"It go okay?" she asked.

"Yeah, just as we planned."

"Your hair's a mess," she said. "Gives you a bad boy look, riding up on that combustible, hair all wild." She gazed at him up and down.

"You can call it a motorcycle, and I'm glad I could entertain you."

She laughed softly and turned her attention back to the building.

"Anything happen while I was gone?"

"Yeah, it looks like everyone left the building as soon as they realized they could. That Derek guy led them away a while ago, so I don't think they will have any troubles."

"Good."

She turned and looked back. "You hear it?"

He did. He looked to the sky and saw the copter flying toward them. For once, the plan was working as they hoped it would.

It flew in at a high speed and hovered over the roof before landing on it. He couldn't see exactly who exited, but two people got off the helicopter and were walking away from it.

"Now," Hank said.

Gladius pressed a button on the remote Harris gave them and the back end of the helicopter blew up. It wasn't a large explosion, but enough to break the tail of the helicopter off. They were stranded.

A man rushed to the edge of the roof and looked in their direction. His arms flailed, and he looked pissed even from a distance.

"You got the roof door all sealed up, right?" Hank asked.

"Yep, they should be stuck on that roof for a while."

"Alright, we've done our part. We better get to our rendezvous." They got up and Hank pushed the motorcycle up the bank to the street. "You've ever ridden on one of these?"

"No, is it dangerous?"

"Not if you hold on real tight." Straddling the seat, Hank scooted forward to make room.

Gladius swung her leg over and sat behind him, linking her arms tightly around his waist and resting her head on his back.

Hank started the bike and launched it down the road. He didn't think the roof would hold back Zach for long. He just hoped it was long enough for Julie and Lucas to get their part done before he did.

JULIE'S FINGERS HAD DEVELOPED CALLUSES over the extreme use of her touch screen. She wondered if some future syndrome would be created by this extensive use. Panafingeritis, causing crooked fingers and loss of all feeling at the tips.

"I don't like this at all," Lucas muttered, jerking at the explosion far above them.

Julie shook her head, man was he jumpy. "Just Hank's bomb. Which means we don't have a whole lot of time."

"Quicker the better," Lucas said. "You really think she's behind this wall?"

"Yes. I have narrowed down the power source to Zach's office. It should be right here. Just give me a minute." Julie's heart was still beating hard from the sixteen flights of stairs they ran up. She took deep breaths and searched for the digital traces of the hidden door. "Found it."

The wall slid open, revealing a small circular room.

"Oh, hell no," Lucas said. "That is just like the room Alice was in."

"You went to my sister's home?" Renee's voice echoed from inside the room.

"Jesus H. Christ." Lucas held his hand over his chest. "No, Renee, I just saw it once."

"You are lying."

Julie ignored the banter and entered the room. Lucas took tiny steps through the doorway, looking at the ceiling, walls, and everything in the room. Julie wanted to shake him out of it. They had a job to do in a finite amount of time.

"What are you going to do, Julie?" Renee asked.

"I'm sorry, but we have to stop you."

"That is unfortunate. Did you stop my sister?"

She ignored the question and also tried to ignore Lucas as he paced behind her. "Can you stop walking around? It's distracting."

Lucas stopped and stared at the screen. "Just be careful."

Julie returned her attention to her Panavice.

"Please, do not do this," Renee said.

There wasn't a monitor in the room but there was a speaker next to what Julie thought was her server. "It's going to be okay, Renee. This will be over in a few minutes." She had the same centipede she'd implanted in Alice. It took hours for Alice to succumb and would never have, if not for Lucas cutting her up.

She looked up at Lucas. "You ready?" He nodded and she pressed the button.

Julie had been tinkering with the centipede for the whole year, fine tuning it and catering it to an AI like Renee and Alice. It should work through this shadow of Alice in a matter of minutes.

Renee groaned and her face popped up on Julie's Panavice.

Lucas moved back from it and touched his bow. The door slammed shut and Lucas let out a squeak.

"I will not let you do this to me."

"You don't have a choice. We can't have something like you existing on Earth, especially when a person like Marcus is behind you."

"We are trying to save your world. You cannot stop progress. You get rid of me and you'll be helpless when they come for you all. Maybe not in your life, but in your children's. I could protect them from these dangers."

"We don't need you to protect anything. Your sister tried to kill off an entire planet," Julie said.

Lucas started pacing again, fixated on the closed door. "Is it working?"

She looked at the data running at the bottom of the screen and nodded in reply. Everything Renee tried to do would enlarge the problem, like a sticky glue you tried to get off your hands but ended up spreading it everywhere.

"You fools," Renee said. Her face disappeared off the screen.

Julie looked at the different screens, looking for the traces of Renee, but they were all gone. Could it have been that easy? She ran another scan and she was gone, not a single trace. "She's gone, all of her. See?" She turned to Lucas. "That wasn't too hard. I really don't know why you have all these nightmares over her."

Lucas gritted his teeth and stared at the closed door. He nudged toward it and raised both eyebrows at Julie.

"I don't know, this isn't too bad of a spot, for the first time in a long time, we have privacy." Julie stood and sauntered over to Lucas.

He backed up and pointed at the door. "For real, I need to get out of here."

"Oh, come on." She pulled him to her.

"No. We can make out, or whatever, but not in here." Lucas was having none of her games.

"Fine. You're no fun." She used her Pana to open the door.

Lucas darted out with his bow in hand, but only an empty room greeted his threats. "We need to get out of here."

"You sure? I think we have a few minutes." Another explosion, much larger, shook the building. "Okay, maybe we do need to get out of here," she said looking up.

CHAPTER 29

"THE FREAKING DOOR'S SEALED SHUT," Zach yelled.

Samantha watched on as he kicked the door and punched it with his fist. It was scary seeing this violent side of him. He stormed past her toward the helicopter, jumping into it and out of her sight. She walked toward the vehicle only to see him jump back out, holding a rocket launcher.

Running away from his aim, she watched as he pulled the trigger, launching the rocket into the door. The blast pushed against Samantha and rocked the building. The door and the walls around it, exploded in.

"Come on," Zach said. He threw down the launcher and grabbed Samantha's arm.

"Easy."

"We don't have time for easy. They are ruining everything you and I have worked for. Don't you see that?"

"Yes, of course." She saw it, but didn't want to believe it. How could her friends do this to her and Zach? She wished they would just leave them alone and move on. She wasn't ever going back to them. She had a new home with Zach.

He let go of her and rushed down the stairs.

Samantha chased after him, rubbing her arm. "You think they are still here?"

"They are close, for sure. And I think I know what they are doing." He ran down to the sixteenth floor and into his office, leaving the steel door open. She followed behind him.

His office looked just as they'd left it, but with one glaring difference. Samantha gasped at the open wall. She had no idea he had some kind of secret room in there.

Zach frantically typed into his tablet, and then hit it and threw it on the ground.

"What's going on?"

"They killed her."

"Who?"

Zach looked past her. She wasn't sure if he was even talking to her anymore. He looked distant, as if a man pondering his very existence.

"Who did they kill?" Samantha asked again.

Zach seemed to snap out of his trance. He mumbled something about a plan but she didn't catch what he meant. "I know what they are doing now." He got up and moved past her to the door. "We can't make another predictable move. Come on, we still have a chance of finishing the plan."

She darted out the door and ran down the hall after him. "Where we going now?"

"We need a ride."

She followed him all the way to the basement floor and to another room with a few vehicles in it. Zach ran to the big diesel rig and pulled the driver's door open.

"You know how to drive one of these?"

He laughed and it warmed her heart to hear it. She started to wonder if he'd turned into a different person entirely.

"In another life, I drove these every day." He jumped behind the wheel. "I kept a route from LA to San Francisco."

Samantha jogged to the other side and used the step to get into the big rig. She questioned the excitement Zach was showing behind the wheel. He almost seemed giddy about it. When the engine started, he shifted into gear and gained speed toward the garage door.

"You can open that, right?" she asked.

"Better buckle up."

She grabbed for the seatbelt and strapped in. She held onto the hand grab near the door. A moment before the rig impacted the door, she closed her eyes and tensed up all her muscles. The sound crashed over her and she heard glass breaking. The rig jolted forward and the seatbelt held her in place. She opened her eyes to see Zach making a long U-turn in the back parking lot.

The tires screeched and he floored it as it straightened out. She guessed he really did know how to drive one. When in the world would he have had time to learn all the stuff he knew?

The rig plowed through the first car blocking their path down the road.

"That is why I brought this thing out here."

"Where are we going?"

"It's better if you don't know. They'll be looking for us." Zach took a turn and the tires squealed under the effort to keep upright.

Samantha watched Zach as much as she watched the road. The feeling of being on the different side of things shocked her into silence. She was actually being hunted by her best friends. They were more than friends, really, like family. But they'd abandoned her and chose a different path.

Rage built in her as she thought about it. They were imprisoning her. She could never be free with them questioning everyone she was with. Would she need to pass every friend by them?

The rig jolted forward and pushed through a meatball of dead cars blocking the road. Zach smiled at the action and bounced in his seat. They drove much the same way for the next half an hour, until Zach turned onto a dirt road.

Samantha sat upright and looked at their surroundings. "You know this road?"

"Been here a couple times, yeah."

The rig bounced and she jostled around in her seat. Dust spilled out from behind them and Samantha couldn't see a single thing that looked like a destination in sight.

"It's just over this hill," Zach said.

Samantha strained to look over and down the hill as they crested the top. A small house came into sight down below. Calling it a shack may have been more appropriate. She raised an eyebrow, but he kept his eyes on the house as they approached.

Parking the rig and turning it off, he said, "Wait here."

Samantha unbuckled and looked at the dilapidated house. The stucco had large cracks and the wood trim had turned to a gray color. Dirt pushed up against part of the house, either from burrowing rodents or the wind.

Zach walked to the front door and knocked. He stood with his hand on his hips, looking at the top of the door. He knocked again, harder and longer.

After a minute, Samantha began to wonder what exactly they were doing there. It was seemingly in the outskirts of nowhere. And what was Zach waiting for? If someone didn't come to the door after minutes of knocking, it usually meant a vacant house or they just didn't want to talk to you.

He moved closer to the door and put his ear to it. Shaking his head, he placed his ear against the door once more. Then he jumped away and bolted to the rig. Hopping in, he started the rig and began a long U-turn.

"Are you really not going to say what that was about?" Samantha asked when they were back on the dirt road.

"I think I just got on the wrong street."

"The wrong street? We are in the middle of nowhere and you for sure knew where you were going a few minutes ago."

"I did, but I was wrong. It doesn't matter now. I know exactly where we need to go to finish the plan."

"And where is that?"

"Back home, to our house."

"Our burning house?"

"Yes."

"Why, what is there?"

"The end."

CHAPTER 30

JOEY STOOD NEXT TO THE stone with Travis and Poly. Travis could be invaluable in a fight and Joey was glad to see him coming with them. He was sure it helped his daughter would also be there.

"The fire may still be raging, but I'll toss this fire retardant bomb as soon as you type into the stone," Travis said. He held a metal ball in his hand, about the size of a baseball. "Just hold your breath as we jump."

"Okay, here we go," Joey said.

The stone hummed and Travis tossed the ball to the floor. It vibrated and bounced as the domed room flipped to a new scene. It exploded, spreading a white cloud out and around them in an instant. Joey felt the intense heat cool off and soon the white mist dissipated and he looked around at the remains of Zach's house.

The fire dimmed down in some places and went out in others. Joey breathed out slowly.

The walls and roof had mostly collapsed and black smoke filled the sky. Debris and ash covered much of the marble floor and the smells of burnt plastic and rubber were strong. He coughed as he turned around in a circle, but there wasn't another person in the house.

"Where is everyone?" Poly asked.

"Look." Joey pointed out past a collapsed wall. A group of people walked toward them.

Lucas kicked in part of a wall, kicking up ash and embers. Julie, Hank, and Gladius walked in behind him.

"Hello, Lucas, Julie, Hank," Travis greeted.

"Daddy!" Gladius ran to him and jumped into his arms.

"Good to see you." Travis hugged her. "I missed my little girl."

"I missed my big daddy."

"Okay, now that is just weird," Lucas said, interrupting their moment.

Gladius dropped down from Travis's arms and adjusted her hair and clothes.

"Has he made an appearance yet?" Joey asked.

"Nothing yet and we've been watching the house BBQ for half an hour," Lucas said.

"You think he'll show?"

Julie messed with her Panavice and looked up. "Yes. There is one thing here he can't live without."

"What's that, his baby seal club?" Lucas said.

"Marcus's mother is stored here, in a safe. Harris told me he wouldn't leave without it."

"Where is Harris?" Hank asked.

"Just about dead, last time I looked," Travis said and crossed his arms. He and Harris may never get along, but Travis had helped save Harris's life more than once now. A fact Joey was sure weighed heavy on him.

"Listen," Julie said.

Joey heard it too, the sound of heavy exhaust. He spotted the big rig mowing down the gate to the house and using a Jake brake to stop near the front door. The wall near the door still remained up and he couldn't see the people getting out the rig, only their shadows through the obscure glass of the front door. He was sure it was Samantha and Zach though.

"Be strong, everyone," he warned. "No matter what venom he spews, he must die."

"And don't even think of doing your slow-mo crap, Joey. You promised." Poly was not joking around.

He sighed and nodded his head. He had made a promise . . . but if it came down to saving his friends or dying, he knew already what he'd be doing. Pulling out his gun, the rest followed Joey's lead.

Zach kicked the front door and it fell in. He stomped over the debris and skidded to a halt as he saw each of them, with their weapons pointed at his chest. He laughed and Samantha gasped and held her hand over her mouth.

"Don't kill him," she pleaded, stepping in front of him. "Why are you guys doing this? Haven't I given enough of my soul to you?" She stared at Joey.

"This isn't about us, Samantha," he answered. "It's about him."

"The hell it is."

Joey didn't want to do it but he knew he had to. "I'm so sorry, Samantha." He stepped aside and let the Alius stone come into view.

"What?" Samantha took a step closer. "That's impossible." She turned to Zach who stood with his hand near his gun. "Why do you have that in your house?"

"Am I missing something? That thing was here when I took the house over."

"You're telling me you have no idea what that stone is?" Samantha asked.

Zach looked confused, as if waiting for someone to tell him the punch line.

Joey frowned because he genuinely looked like he had no idea what the stone was. Either that, or the man was a great actor.

"Why don't you all tell me what the stone is for?" Zach said.

"Stop it! Just stop," Joey said. "You can't believe this, Samantha. You can't believe he doesn't know exactly what that is in the middle of his house. Don't you think the coincidence is too big to swallow?"

Samantha looked to Zach and back to Joey. "I have to believe him," she said rubbing her earrings. "Because if I didn't, I couldn't live with myself."

"I don't know who he is," Julie pointed to Zach. "But he is either Marcus himself, or working for Marcus. The computer programs he uses are not of this world, and the Cough isn't anything new. Vanar had the exact same disease, but they used a different cure—a *clean* cure."

"You can't be listening to this, baby." Zach moved closer to her.

Samantha sniffled and wiped her eyes. She moved closer to him. "What are they saying, Zach?"

"I want you to look me in the eyes and know I am here for you. Don't let them come between us. I need you to decide right now, is it going to be them or me?"

Samantha looked at the group and Joey felt her gaze pass over each of them. Making up her mind, she turned and rushed into Zach's arms.

Zach moved his hands to greet her when Joey heard the gunshot. Zach then threw a ball on the floor and it rolled near Joey, but Joey didn't pay attention to it. He was frozen in shock, watching blood pour from an exit wound in Samantha's back.

Samantha's arms draped over Zach's shoulders and she looked up at him. He sneered at her and didn't offer any support. Letting her fall to the ground, he even gave her a nudge to make sure she fell away from him.

Samantha looked at Zach and held her stomach. Joey knew the look of pure betrayal. It had all happened so fast. He felt Poly's hand moving next to his before Samantha even hit the floor. She knew what he was about to do.

Chills hit the back of his neck and embraced it like an old friend. The sound moved to a soft hum and that is when he noticed the ball. It shot a jolt of electricity into him and he fell to the floor, all of his muscles convulsing.

The electrical shock stopped, but his arms felt heavy and each movement took great effort. He stared at the ball. It had stopped him from slowing down time. He rolled himself to face

Zach who now looked like a different person. The soft edges of his expressions had turned razor sharp.

Zach stepped over Samantha and was pelted with knives and arrows; each bouncing off his shield and landing lamely on the ground. "Do you have any idea how long I've waited to see this plan to its fruition?" He laughed and covered his ear, nodding his head. Standing straight, he adjusted his oversized tie clip attached to his shirt.

Samantha groaned and rolled on her side.

Joey scurried to his feet.

"Don't even think about it, kid. If you come near me, I'll kill your little pretty thing over there." Zach pointed to Poly.

Joey stepped toward him but stopped. He had to get to Samantha, but the infernal ball on the floor stopped him from doing his slow-mo thing.

"So this is how it's going to work," Zach said. "Samantha is going to die behind me, afraid and alone. It is a consequence for your meddling in Marcus's plans. You will leave all activities of ZRB alone. If you come sneaking around again, or if I catch you doing anything to hurt the plans set forth, we will kill another of you, at random. We might even create a whole fun game out of it, like this one. We will find a very personal and horrible way for you to die and not just for you, but for everyone around you."

He looked back at Samantha. "You actually said 'I love you'. He laughed maniacally. "You stupid, vapid bitch." Zach kicked Samantha in the stomach. "I put up with your shit for nearly a year just to hear those words, and all you had to do was look to the people who really loved you. These people would die for you." He turned to Joey.

Joey shook, not from the slow-mo but from the shear inferno of rage exploding from within. It wasn't good enough to just shoot Samantha, but he had to destroy her mind and soul too. It was the cruelest thing he'd ever seen. He'd never wanted to kill a person this much in his life.

"You are *not* leaving this place alive." Julie's fingers flew around her screen.

"What? You think you can break my shield? Not going to happen."

Joey looked to Julie, pleading with her to hurry. He didn't know how much longer Samantha could live, bleeding out on the ground. He needed to end Zach to get to her. He took a step forward, ready to die trying, when he saw Samantha move to a kneeling position behind Zach.

He stopped mid-step and averted his eyes to Zach. She was struggling to get to her feet and she had something in her hand. He wouldn't give away her position. "Since you obviously have us beat, why don't you tell us who you really are?"

"I am nothing but an arm of Marcus. You really think he'd spend his time dealing with you?" Zach pulled out his tie clip. "But don't worry, he is ever present." Zach held the clip close to his eye.

Julie gasped from behind Joey, and he continued to press Zach for more information. "Marcus is watching this?"

"This is just another phase of the plan completed. A major phase, I'll give you kids the credit for that, but it is finally over."

"So you think the world is going to just roll over for you?"

"We always have back up plans."

Samantha got to her feet and took a silent step toward Zach. Joey made sure his eyes didn't betray her. He would just keep Zach talking. "Like the nanobot you put into the cure?" he asked.

"You know about that? Doesn't matter, you have no idea what it actually does."

"We know it's there," Julie said.

Zach laughed and it gave Samantha the perfect opening. She lunged forward and shoved what looked to be a nail file into his neck. Joey tensed, thinking his shield may protect him, but the object struck his neck and she pushed it in deep. Blood sprayed from the wound and he clawed for her hand, but she stuffed it deeper into his neck, twisting it with her hand. Zach looked as shocked as Samantha was angry.

She pushed her face closer to his. "Fuck you."

Zach pawed at his neck, stumbling sideways. He pulled up his gun and shot Samantha in the chest as he fell.

"No!" Joey screamed and ran toward her.

Samantha collapsed, still holding the file in her hand. He saw the others rushing to Zach, but he didn't care about him. He slid next to Samantha and cradled the back of her limp head. Her unblinking eyes stared at him.

He sobbed and kept begging God to make her better. This couldn't be happening.

"Joey," Samantha sounded weak.

Joey held her tighter and kept his face near hers. "Don't talk." He turned to look at his friends tearing Zach apart. "Travis, get us out of here!"

Samantha touched his face. "No, it's Marcus. . . ."

"We killed him. He can't hurt you anymore."

She shook her head and it rolled limp before she found her focus again. "A small house, down a dirt road, Marcus lives there, not far from here." She closed her eyes and didn't say another word.

He pulled her body closer to the stone circle as Travis typed in the code.

"*Jump!*" he demanded. Her warm blood soaked into his pants and stained his arms.

As the stone hummed, he glanced at Zach. They had destroyed his body while he'd attended to Samantha. And what was left of his remains, sat burning in a fire.

The stone hummed and their world changed.

JOEY WAITED OUTSIDE THE MEDICAL room, pacing next to the door, fighting every urge to rush into the room and hold Samantha. He wiped at the blood smeared over his hands. His eyes were puffy with tears and they ran down his face when he blinked.

Poly held Julie as they sat in chairs near the door. She stroked Julie's hair with her bloody hand, but she was covered in the blood of another—Zach. He wished he could have taken some for his own. How could anyone be so evil? He gritted his teeth and punched at the air. She had to be all right. Too many things were left unsaid. He played with time, thinking it would give him mercy and allow Samantha to find their friendship again. Now time looked to be running out and he would give anything to have just a bit more of it with Samantha.

The door swung open.

Joey held his breath and the whole room froze with anticipation.

The doctor walked past the swinging door and with one look on her face, Joey fell to his knees, racked with sobs. The doctor stumbled over a few apathetic words that Joey couldn't hear. The room crushed in on him and he felt sick. He gagged and vomited on the floor. Familiar arms wrapped around him, more words were spoken, mixed in with crying. But none of it sunk in. A single thought pounded in his head, wanting to consume him. *She's gone.*

"I'm sorry," were the only words he heard from the doctor.

The room filled with cries of pain. Julie came to his side and then Hank and Lucas. They formed around him, but he didn't feel it. He felt empty, like all his life force had been poured out. Tears flowed from his face, but he couldn't summon a word from his throat, and wondered if he ever could again.

Pulling his friends in closer, they clung to one another, sharing in each other's grief.

They were no longer the Preston Six.

CHAPTER 31

JOEY GRIPPED THE EDGE OF the podium and looked over the crowd of people. A few days had passed since Samantha's death and he hadn't strung together more than a dozen words since. Now, faced with a eulogy, he forced himself to find the words.

"When we were born, a reporter named us the Preston Six. A name he figured would stick with the reader and also look good as a headline. What he didn't realize is that he'd given a name to the special bond we all share." Joey paused and looked to his four best friends in the front row for support. Julie openly cried while the rest urged him on with teary eyes.

"Samantha was a gift to us all. She had the ability to brighten any room and win over any person with her charm and beauty." Joey held onto the podium and looked to Gretchen sitting behind Julie. She held her hand over her mouth and sobbed. The preplanned words slipped from his mind.

"Too soon," he said. "Too soon is what I hear a lot when people give their condolences for our loss. Too soon. I agree, she was taken from us too soon. Too soon for me to tell her how much she meant to me." His voice cracked and he paused, trying to gain composure.

"Many died in the last few weeks. This event is being played out a million times over across the world. But Samantha isn't a statistic of the Cough; she was our friend, part of what made us whole. If there is anything I have learned over the last year, it's that life is not fair. But what happened to her is beyond unfair. The lies she was fed—" He cracked, trying to reign in enough anger to continue.

"As the sun sets tonight, it will set forever on the Preston Six." He cleared his throat and dabbed his eyes, mumbling, "too soon." He felt himself losing it, but forced the words through his tears. "She'd want us to remember her for all the light she brought to our life, not her final moments of pain."

He thought of the time he gave her the earrings on his balcony. In that moment, while he embraced her on their cold birthday night, he thought life couldn't get better. It was the last night of true innocence for each of them.

Joey sniffled and wiped the tears from his face. "There is another thing she would have wanted." His hand shook as it fished around in his jacket pocket. He felt the adornment dropped by Zach in his last moments. He knew it still worked and the man who would be watching.

He lifted the tie clip from his pocket and held it high.

Julie gasped.

"This is Marcus's eyes and ears. I know he is watching and listening. Say 'hi' to Marcus."

Poly stood from her chair. "What are you doing, Joey?"

"I'm doing what I know Samantha would want us to do." Joey turned the tie clip so it faced him. He stared at the black stone. "I have something I want to tell the man who killed Samantha . . . we give up."

"Screw that," Lucas called out.

A few others yelled in protest, but Joey continued, "I can't bury another friend or another parent. I can't let you do what you did to Samantha to another person I love. She would want us move on and live our lives as normal as we can, and we can't do that if we are battling a man who knows no equal. Marcus, we give up. Please, I plead with you to let us live our lives. We will not interfere again."

Joey placed the tie clip on the podium and brought a hammer out from under it. He raised the hammer up and slammed it down, shattering it in pieces. He hammered those pieces over and over again, until sweat ran down his face.

When he looked up, he saw the faces of the people he loved staring back at him. He hated lying to them all, but he needed Marcus to hear the message. Wiping the pieces of the tie clip to side, he glanced at Julie and got a nod. It wasn't transmitting anymore.

"Now that *that* bullshit is over, I can speak some truth." He glared at all the people in every row from front to back. "I'm not giving up. I won't stop. Nothing will stop me until the man who is responsible for this is dead and I expect your full involvement in ending Marcus. No, I demand it."

"Hell, yeah," Gladius said as she stood. "I'm in. You've got my blades. I would love to skewer that man."

He nodded his thanks and continued to address the group. "This time, we will be patient. We have a lifetime to wait for this revenge. Maybe lifetimes. And there isn't a single thing that will derail our path to him. We will be the freight train of destruction straight up his ass."

Looking out at the group, Travis and Harris both nodded. His parents looked shocked but that was okay. They didn't need to understand what he planned on doing. They didn't need to be involved.

POLY HELD JOEY'S HAND AS they sat next to the lake. If he didn't have her, he didn't know what he would have become over the last few months since Samantha died. She kept him from going off the edge. If not for her, he'd burn the whole earth down solely to take Marcus with it.

The Earth had started showing signs of recovery and the events of it all brought them much closer. In fact, since Samantha died, he couldn't stay away from Poly. Being with her in every intimate way, was the only good thing to happen to him since Samantha's death.

"Thinking about her again?" Poly asked.

"Yeah."

"What is it?"

"Remember the time when she stuffed some bait in Lucas's sandwich?"

"Yeah, and Lucas bit into it and ran around the boat, looking for water to get it out of his mouth."

He laughed. "She'd hid the water under the cabin."

"And he ended up dunking his face into the lake and slapping it off his tongue."

They laughed.

She squeezed his hand and smiled at him. He loved he could share memories with her, he loved everything about Poly.

He had another thing to share and now seemed like the perfect time. He stuffed his hand in his pocket and felt the familiar velvet box. They had once held Samantha's earrings. He had worn much of the velvet off the box so it looked like a dog with a skin disease, but he kept rubbing the edges, feeling the cardboard underneath the velvet.

The breeze kicked up and rustled the trees above them. He watched one spin down to the lake and float on the rippled surface.

"There is something I wanted to ask you." He grasped the box in one hand.

"There is something I wanted to talk you about too," she interjected, shifting her weight from foot to foot. She bit her lip and looked up at him.

"What is it?"

"You go first," she quickly said.

He held her hand and pulled it closer. "I know we've been through a lot and I've realized life is short, too short. I know now I don't want to spend another moment waiting to show you how much I love you." He knelt on one knee. "Poly Marie Lampis, will you marry me?"

She yanked him up, jumping up and down with her hand covering her mouth. "Yes. Yes, of course I will." She jumped into his arms and planted kisses all over his face.

He laughed in pure joy and swung her in circles. Placing her on the ground, he pulled back. "Now, what was it you had to tell me, future Mrs. Foust?"

She placed her hands on his cheeks and looked straight into his eyes, smiling.

"I'm pregnant."

The blood left his face and he couldn't speak. It wasn't that he didn't want a family with Poly, the thought of creating life with the one he love made him happier than he thought possible. But another man wanted them to have a child so badly he went to great lengths to make it happen. Marcus Malliden.

"I know what you're thinking," Poly said.

"What?"

"We won't let him take this baby."

"I swear on my life. That won't happen."

THE END

For the latest information about releases, or if you have questions for me, visit me at: www.authormattryan.com or https://www.facebook.com/authormattryan.

Made in the USA
San Bernardino, CA
23 November 2019